THE
CALLING

THE
CALLING

ROD CONNELL

TATE PUBLISHING
AND **ENTERPRISES**, LLC

Published by Tate Publishing & Enterprises, LLC
127 E. Trade Center Terrace | Mustang, Oklahoma 73064 USA
1.888.361.9473 | www.tatepublishing.com

Tate Publishing is committed to excellence in the publishing industry. The company reflects the philosophy established by the founders, based on Psalm 68:11,
"The Lord gave the word and great was the company of those who published it."

Book design copyright © 2014 by Tate Publishing, LLC. All rights reserved.
Cover design by Eileen Cueno
Interior design by Jomar Ouano

Published in the United States of America

ISBN: 978-1-63418-141-9
Religion / Christian Life / General
14.10.02

To the One who has called His own back to Himself, drawing us by His great love, from before the foundation of the world…who, in spite of our many failures and unworthiness, has called us to share in His glory, now and forevermore!

Contents

INTRODUCTION

The most basic question that all mankind must answer is *why in the world am I here?* What is the purpose of my existence? Many quite consciously seek an answer to this question. Others do not, but the very way in which they live their lives bears witness to their answer: they live from day to day, striving as best they can, garnering as much pleasure and happiness that this life has to offer but never really looking beyond that. They never seek God for an answer.

And yet it is only our Maker who has the answer. He not only has the answer but has been quite eager to give it! The intention of this book is to thoroughly explore what God has to say on the subject, for His answer is both multifaceted and marvelous.

A good place to start is the most simple and direct answer to the question, which is to be found in the *Westminster Confession of Faith*, compiled in Scotland in 1646–48. This document was originally written to ground children in the Christian faith, using a question-answer format, so the first question asked and answered was *what is the chief end of man?* The answer: *to glorify God and enjoy Him forever*—how simple and yet profound!

But of course, to glorify and enjoy God, we must first come to know Him. So the initial move is on the part of God: He must reveal Himself—which He has so graciously done in the Bible, in what has become known as the Word of God to mankind. To that end, He has called men unto Himself, making a way through His Holy Spirit for us to see and receive His goodness and glory, for us to indeed know by experience the ample reasons to glorify and enjoy Him forever!

So come along, let us embark on this remarkable journey together that we might come to know and experience the answer to all our questions surrounding the basic one: *why in the world am I here?*

CALLED

Throughout the entire history of Christianity, being "called" by God has been a much debated issue. First of all, what does it mean? And called to what? Is everyone called? Some believe that everyone is not, that the verse in Matthew 22:14 ("many are called, but few chosen") means God is quite selective in whom He calls, passing over some in favor of others. But if this were so, even human thought could bring a charge of unfairness against God.

The much-loved scripture of John 3:16 declares God "so loved *the world* that He gave His only begotten Son," the whole world and everyone in it. God's call is indeed for everyone. The problem is that not everyone responds to the call. Oswald Chambers in *My Utmost for His Highest* puts it like this: "Whether I hear God's call or not depends on the condition of my ears, and exactly what I hear depends on my spiritual condition." So the number one reason of *why in the world am I here?* is to hear and respond to the call of God, about which Chambers goes on to say: "The chosen ones are those who have come into a relationship with God through Jesus Christ and have had their [spiritual] ears opened."

Therefore, the primary purpose of our life is to find God, to hear Him, and to respond in faith; put another way, to *seek* Him, for the Scripture assures us "that without faith it is impossible to please Him, for he who comes to God must believe that He is, and that He is a rewarder of those who diligently seek Him" (Hebrews 11:6).

Blessed is the man who turns from the temporary idols and concerns of this world and seeks after those things that are eternal, to which God has called everyone.

CALLED TO SALVATION

For all have sinned and fall short of the glory of God.

Romans 3:23

For the wages of sin is death, but the gift of God is eternal life in Christ Jesus our Lord.

Romans 6:23

Nevertheless I tell you the truth. It is to your advantage that I go away; for if I do not go away, the Helper will not come to you; but if I depart, I will send him to you. And when He has come, He will convict the world of sin, and of righteousness, and of judgment: of sin, because they do not believe in Me; of righteousness, because I go to My Father and you see me no more; of judgment, because the ruler of this world is judged.

John 16:7–11

I will give you a new heart and put a new spirit within you; I will take the heart of stone out of your flesh and give you a heart of flesh. I will put My Spirit within you and cause you to walk in My statutes, and you will keep My judgments and do them.

Ezekiel 36:26–27

> Blessed are the pure in heart, for they shall see God.
>
> Matthew 5:8

As mentioned earlier, it is God who must make the first move if we are to respond to His call and begin to seek Him. (Praise His holy name; He has indeed done His part!) For we are all born as sinners, offspring of Adam, far from the presence and knowledge of God. Our spirits nonfunctional and our hearts darkened, we do what is right in our own eyes, independent of divine counsel. This was the result of the curse of original sin and the lot of all mankind until the coming of Christ.

God's answer to man's plight was to send His own Son in the flesh to defeat Satan, sin, and death, thereby making a way back to Himself. Jesus's perfect life, death on the cross, and resurrection, all in our place and on our behalf, have accomplished God's purpose. But this magnificent event and fact must be appropriated by each individual to become effectual.

Enter the Holy Spirit! For it is the work of the Spirit that makes Christ, His great work and sacrifice real to each individual heart. So the first step for the Holy Spirit is to give a child of Adam a new heart. The natural-born, old heart is a heart of stone, Ezekiel tells us (36:26), as hard as the stone tablets Moses received on Mount Sinai. The old law could not produce righteousness nor a new heart. Man, in his own power, could never find his way back to God.

So, as Ezekiel foretold, the Holy Spirit gives a new heart, no longer darkened and unable to receive the words of God, but alive and sensitive to the light the Spirit next sends. That light is the word of conviction, whereby the sinner realizes his wretched condition before a Holy God.

In John 16:7–11, Jesus tells His disciples that He must leave them so He can send the Holy Spirit (for the next phase of the salvation process) to convict the world of sin, righteousness, and judgment. The new quickened heart and conscience are enabled to understand and receive this three-point indictment: the realization of sin and separation from God, no longer relying on any form of self-righteousness; the sight of the true and only righteousness accepted by God (the righteousness of Christ); and the knowledge that only judgment awaits unless there is repentance and belief in the gospel message.

This is the moment of regeneration! For as the unbeliever does indeed repent and believe in the atoning death of Christ on the cross, their dead spirit is quickened to life by the Holy Spirit; he is given a new spirit, even as Ezekiel prophesied. Thus we have what Jesus called being born again or born from above (John 3:3). The new spirit is now able to receive and understand the scriptures as they are imparted by the Holy Spirit, and the new heart is inflamed by a deep love for the Lord and spiritual truth, desiring only to follow Christ wherever He might lead.

But the work of the Holy Spirit does not stop there! He also indwells the new believer to guide, instruct, and empower the newborn child of God in his walk of maturing in Christ. For the flesh continues to war with the Spirit throughout the life of a believer, and without the indwelling Holy Spirit, there is no way to victory in this struggle. The believer must learn and be willing to walk as Jesus walked, surrendering his own will to the will of Christ, even as Christ always submitted to the will of the Father. This is an ongoing, lifelong process of sanctification, the work of the Word (sword of the Spirit), the cross, and the

Holy Spirit, with the goal of conforming the believer to the image of Christ.

Indeed, regeneration, salvation, and sanctification are marvelous transformations! The scriptures refer to the result as a "new creation" and declares that behold, all things become new! My way of understanding this phenomenon is that the creation of man as God originally intended is at last complete. The Father had a plan; Jesus came to carry out the work of the plan, and the Holy Spirit has been at work throughout to ensure the success of the plan. In the process, God's eternal purpose of His Son being all in all and the sum of all things will be accomplished. Of course, I realize that all three members of the Godhead have been involved from beginning to end, each with a unique role for the common purpose to be realized, all of this inherent in the great mystery of the Trinity.

What else is there to say or do but shout hallelujah and fall on our face in adoration and praise!

(Note: What follows are the many other callings upon our life, those that follow the call, and our response to the call to salvation. These callings are not in any particular order, progressive, nor by order of importance, and the list is certainly not all-inclusive or exhaustive. I have simply chosen those as prompted by the Holy Spirit.)

CALLED TO EXPERIENCE GOD'S LOVE

Beloved, let us love one another, for love is of God; and everyone who loves is born of God and knows God. He who does not love is not of God, for [*God is love*].

1 John 4:7–8)

We love Him because He first loved us.

1 John 4:19

The Lord is not slack concerning His promises, as some count slackness, but is longsuffering toward us, not willing that any should perish but that all should come to repentance.

2 Peter 3:19

After we have responded to God's call to salvation and are reborn, what is the next thing He calls us to do? Most of us start with many false ideas about God and what He expects of us. We might think of a long list of dos and don'ts, for example, what will please Him and what will not. And while God does indeed care about our behavior, that is not His primary concern in our relationship in the beginning of our walk, nor should it be ours.

As newborn believers, we are called first of all to experience His love. For His love is unlike any other; it so extravagant that it defies words to describe it! We call it *agape* in an effort to distinguish it from the three lower forms of love, and *agape* is defined as selfless, sacrificial love, etcetera. But the love of God soars so far beyond the definition of a single word that it will take all eternity to plumb its heights and depths. Each new day in the kingdom and the new heaven and earth will bring fresh revelations of God's limitless love!

Of such love, of course, we can only experience a small portion while yet in this body of flesh. But we can experience enough to fill and fortify us against all the rigors of this life and the wiles of our ancient foe, the devil. The book of Hebrews calls it a "taste of the age to come" (6:5). And Romans 8:37–39 assures us that "in all these things, we are more than conquerors through Him who loved us. For I am persuaded that neither death nor life, nor angels nor principalities nor powers, nor things present nor things to come, nor height nor depth, nor any other created thing, shall be able to separate us from the love of God which is in Christ Jesus our Lord."

God is the very author of love, and we love Him because He first loved us (1 John 4:19). Love is indeed the very nature of God, all His other divine attributes branching out from that central core. Everything He does is motivated by love (counterbalanced by His justice of course). So it is critical that we experience His love, and that it becomes our motivating factor as well, our very way of life: love God, love ourselves, and love others. First John 4:8 makes it clear that love is the very gauge of whether we even know God or not: no love, no knowledge.

Many know mentally that God loves them (after all, He sent His Son to die for us), but they do not actively experience it and live it. I had a very interesting experience the other night. I went to sleep thinking about how I could ever describe the love of God, to confine it to words. It seemed quite impossible. About 2:00 a.m., I woke up with that still on my mind. Different descriptions presented themselves, laden with superlative adjectives. But they all seemed so deficient, and I remember being frustrated. But then suddenly the Lord reminded me of my earlier waking thoughts that there is no way to adequately define His love. And with that came peace. Then it seemed that the Lord said, "Just be quiet now and enjoy My love." For the next two hours, I was enwrapped by the most rapturous waves of glory! The Spirit was trying to tell me, "This *is* the love of God," and the entire next day, the remnants of that experience stayed with me, none of the nettlesome things of the day bothering me in the least.

Of course, the love of God is much more than just these high mountaintop times. There are also valleys, even wildernesses, to pass through, times when the Lord seems far off, times of dryness and struggle. But once His love is experienced, there is a quiet confidence, faith, and hope that carry us through. For with His love comes the sustaining assurance that whatever comes our way from His hand is for our good and His glory. It is all a process of conforming us to the image of Christ (more on this later); the cross must do its work in our life if we are to reach the pinnacle of our calling.

So much more could be, and will be, written on the love of God as we make the rest of our journey together. But for now, it is my sincere prayer that all of you who are reading these lines will stop and take time to truly seek and experience the love of the Lord. It will change everything!

It will cause you to love Him all the more, to be more like Him. It will deepen your commitment to Him, help clarify His purpose for your life. And it will release more victory over sin. For His great love will *constrain* (2 Corinthians 5:14) you, so that your greatest desire will be to please Him who has done so much for you. Hallelujah and amen!

CALLED TO FREEDOM

If you abide in My word, you are My disciples indeed. And you shall know the truth, and the truth shall make you free...Most assuredly, I say to you, whoever commits sin is a slave of sin...Therefore if the Son makes you free, you shall be free indeed.

John 8:31, 32, 34, 36

The Spirit of the Lord is upon Me, because He has anointed Me to preach the gospel to the poor; He has sent Me to heal the brokenhearted, to proclaim liberty to the captives and recovery of sight to the blind, to set at liberty those who are oppressed; to proclaim the acceptable year of the Lord.

Luke 4:18

Now the Lord is the Spirit; and where the Spirit of the Lord is, there is liberty.

2 Corinthians 3:17

Knowing this, that our old man was crucified with Him, that the body of sin might be done away with, that we should no longer be slaves of sin...Likewise you also, reckon yourselves to be dead indeed to sin, but alive to God in Christ Jesus our Lord.

Romans 6:6, 11

> There is therefore now no condemnation to those
> who are in Christ Jesus, who do not walk according
> to the flesh, but according to the Spirit. For the law
> of the Spirit of life in Christ Jesus has made me free
> from the law of sin and death.

Romans 8:1–2

We all enter life as prisoners, whether we know it or not. In fact, we don't realize it for a long time. We live life doing the best we can, not knowing that there is anything wrong. We make ourselves as comfortable as possible, with all sorts of plans and dreams, obeying the laws of the land as best we can, working hard to succeed. But then the Holy Spirit enters the picture.

At first, we don't know what it is, but a vague dissatisfaction begins to arise within us. None of the old pleasures and pastimes satisfies us anymore. We may try new ones for awhile, but it is not long before they lose their charm as well. Like the question in the old song, we too begin to ask, *Is this all there is?*

We then begin to feel faint guilt and conviction about some of those pleasures we indulged in. We knew at the time they weren't good things to be doing, but quickly excused ourselves and forgot all about the moral lapses involved. But now, the Holy Spirit begins to deepen our sense of sin. We may have attended church before (or not), so the Holy Spirit uses whatever means it takes to point us to Jesus. Something about His message seems different: the Word penetrates our very heart, and we reach out in faith and repentance, finding Him waiting there with love and forgiveness.

Of course, everybody's story is different, but all the essential elements are the same. The good news reaches the heart and quickens the spirit to life. Christ's forgiveness for the penalty of sin produces great joy and satisfaction! We indeed feel like we have been set free, no longer condemned to judgment, hell, and eternal separation from God, heading some day to heaven. For a long time, we just bathe in the love of God, sailing along on the wings of glory.

This does not last a lifetime, however. As we begin our walk with the Lord, we throw everything we have into it. We never miss church, we read our Bible and pray daily, we witness everywhere we go, we tithe, and volunteer to serve in some ministry of our church. All goes well for quite awhile. But then, once again, the Holy Spirit intervenes.

Most of our old ways we have left behind, the sins of the past not only forgiven but practiced no more. And yet, certain ones try to resurface, which we do our best to resist. Plus, the Holy Spirit points out new areas of failure to attend to. Resistance and exercising our will works for a while; we are able to succeed most of the time. But then comes failure; the resistance of will power is just not enough. And some of the "good" things we used to thrive on now become boring and neglected. We become discouraged, even distraught. We pray and we fast, but to no avail. The words of the old song return: *is this all there is?* In a word, we are stuck. Freed from our original prison cell, but now confined to another.

Of course, if we do not give up, the Holy Spirit will not leave us in such a condition. Little by little (or perhaps all at once!), He will show us that though we have been freed from the penalty of sin, we are yet captive to its power. This is precisely where the apostle Paul found himself in Romans 7.

We find him there, saying, "For what I am doing, I do not understand. For what I will to do, that I do not practice; but what I hate, that I do" (verse 15). He knows that his "old man," who loved to sin, is dead (Romans 6:6), and yet he keeps failing to walk as he knows he should. Sound familiar?

Every sincere believer, sooner or later, will reach this point. Like Paul, we may even cry out, "O wretched man that I am! Who will deliver me from this body of death?" (verse 24). If you are there now, or have been there, know that there is an answer! The Holy Spirit Himself came to Paul's rescue, and will come to yours as well. The revelation? Romans 8:1–2 (italics mine): "There is therefore now no condemnation to those who are in Christ Jesus, who do not walk according to the flesh, but according to the Spirit. *For the law of the Spirit of life in Christ Jesus has made me free from the law of sin and death.*" Hallelujah!

The first thing to notice is that there are two laws involved: the law of sin and death (the law that original sin imprisons everyone from birth) and the law of the Spirit of life (ushered in by Christ's victory over sin, death, and Satan). The only thing that can overcome a law (and not merely hinder its operation) is a higher law, and that is exactly what Christ has placed inside the spirit of every born-again believer. For He Himself has come there to abide! Colossians 1:27 calls it, "Christ in you, the hope of glory." Christ is now a life-giving spirit (1 Corinthians 15:45), and the life (and law!) by which He lives within us is none other than the law of the Spirit of life!

So we not only have eternal life but abundant life as well. By being "in Christ" from before the foundation of the world (Ephesians 1:4–5), when He was crucified, so was our old man (Romans 6:6). By Christ dying in our place, we were freed from the penalty of sin. But the power of sin also had to be overcome, and this has been accomplished by Christ being "in us." It is His life that we must allow to live and be released, for He has already overcome the law of sin and death for us. Did you get that!

That is why Paul says in 1 Corinthians 15:31, "I die daily." His old man he knew to be dead, and his new man, the life of Christ, he knew could not sin. So who was the culprit working so hard to keep the law of the Spirit of life from manifesting? Self, the flesh, a very powerful force that wars with the Spirit, and the Spirit with it (Galatians 5:17) even after regeneration. The flesh is what we must determine to die to daily. And of course, the flesh includes all we were born with naturally: a body and a soul.

The soul, with its will, mind and emotions, is what controlled our life before coming to Christ; the soul was in charge (what we felt, thought, and decided). But once our spirit is quickened to life, it is to be in charge. For in our spirit and heart is where Christ abides, and as we receive and release His Life by the transmission of the Holy Spirit to our spirit, the law of the Spirit of life comes forth. But anytime we allow the soul to lead the way, even with the best of intentions, failure results. For the soul is flesh, and flesh can never give birth to Spirit (John 3:6).

The soul is quite essential in spiritual life, however, for it is to be the steward of what is received from the spirit. The mind must understand, the emotions kept under control, and the will exercised to carry out what the Holy Spirit is communicating. But because the soul was in control for so long, it is very difficult for it to descend to its proper place. It takes the work of the cross to cut away the dross and refine its operation. That is the "dying daily" Paul speaks of: surrendering our will to the will of Christ, so that we might know His will, and then allow His life to come forth for the situation at hand (which usually will require us "doing something"—the carrying out of His will, not just passively waiting for Him to do it for us!).

I did not intend to get into such a prolonged explanation, but felt it necessary so that we might understand how we have been freed from the power, as well as the penalty of sin. And that, my friends, is true freedom! I am not teaching sinless perfection or any such thing. We still sin, but we don't have to! That is what I am trying to say. But when we do sin (which should be less and less as we mature!), we have an advocate with the Father, even Christ, who will forgive us when we confess and repent, and who will cleanse from all unrighteousness (1 John 1:9)!

True freedom in Christ, from both the penalty and power of sin, carries with it so many auxiliary freedoms: the freedom from judgment, the freedom from condemnation, the freedom from the flesh, the freedom from fear, the freedom from doubt and confusion, just to mention a few. And with our freedom come joy unspeakable and full of glory, peace that passes understanding, true patience, steadfastness, love, mercy, and grace toward our brothers and sisters in the Lord; and love and compassion for all those around us who have not come to Christ. And the best of all? Freedom to love and worship the Lord as never before, knowing deeper and deeper realms of love await us, now and in all eternity! (Of course, an exhaustive list of all the benefits of freedom in Christ would require an entire book to cover.) Hallelujah! Free indeed!

CALLED TO HIS BODY AND FAMILY

His Body

For as we have many members in one body, but all the members do not have the same function, so we, being many, are one body in Christ, and individually members of one another."

Romans 12:3–4

And He put all things under His feet, and gave Him to be head over all things to the church, which is His body, the fullness of Him who fills all in all.

Ephesians 1:22–23

For we are members of His body, of His flesh and of His bones.

Ephesians 5:30

And He is the head of the body, the church, who is the beginning, the firstborn from the dead, that in all things He may have the preeminence.

Colossians 1:18

His Family

Jesus said to her, "Do not cling to Me, for I have not yet ascended to My Father; but go to My brethren and say to them, 'I am ascending to My Father and your Father, and go to My God and your God.'"

John 20:17

For as many as are led by the Spirit of God, these are the sons of God. For you did not receive the spirit of bondage again to fear, but you received the Spirit of adoption by whom we cry out, "Abba, Father." The Spirit Himself bears witness with our spirit that we are the children of God.

Romans 8:14–16

Having predestined us to adoption as sons by Jesus Christ to Himself, according to the good pleasure of His will.

Ephesians 1:5

The body of Christ is a great mystery that God is gradually unfolding. Some things we know while others are yet to be revealed. As John said in his first letter, "Beloved, now we are children of God, and it has not yet been revealed what we shall be, but we know that when He is revealed, we shall be like Him, for we shall see Him as He is" (1 John 3:2). We know by this verse and the ones above that body, family, and church are one. Individually, we are members of His family and His church, but collectively, members of His body, of which He is the head. What a calling!

As members of His family, we are loved as sons and daughters. We have been adopted through the blood of

Christ to be the Lord's own brothers and sisters, known as *brethren* in the scriptures. As brethren, we are also heirs and joint-heirs with Christ.(Romans 8:17). All that is His except His deity is ours! We will rule and reign with Him in the millennial kingdom. And even now, spiritually speaking, where He is, we are! (Ephesians 2:1–7). Like all mankind since the Garden of Eden, we were orphans, but no more, for we are the adopted children of God, members of His own family!

The church is to be the *home* of the family, the local gathering or coming together, where the life of Christ is manifest. In the natural process, family members share the same DNA, a similar genetic makeup. In the family of God, all members share the indwelling life of Christ: "To them God willed to make known what are the riches of the glory of this mystery among the Gentiles: which is Christ in you, the hope of glory" (Colossians 1:25–27). In fact, Christ is the firstborn of a new race of mankind, the creation of what God had in mind from before the foundations of the world, a plan subverted in the Garden of Eden.

That is surely the explanation for God declaring *after* the resurrection and not in Bethlehem at His natural birth, "You are My Son, today I have begotten You" (Psalms 2:7, Hebrews 1:5, Acts 13:33). And in 1 Corinthians 15:47–49, Paul speaks of Adam as the first man and Christ as the second. It was not until after the resurrection that the Father had what He had been looking for. With the defeat of Satan and death, all limitations caused by sin had been removed, making way for the culmination of God's original intention and plan. Christ was indeed the firstborn of many brethren, the progenitor of a new race!

By sharing Christ's spiritual DNA by virtue of His indwelling life, His body, family, and church are to be perfect expressions of Christ on the earth. That is our calling. But to accomplish that marvelous goal, like John the Baptist said, we must decrease so that Christ might increase. All vestiges of flesh must be sacrificed and overcome in favor of the Christ within. Our will must be in submission to His will, even as His will was always submitted to the will of the Father. To find our true self, (soul) we must lose the false one, the one which had been in control of our life before we came to Christ. Our newborn spirit must follow the Holy Spirit, with our soul (mind, will, and emotions) no longer leading the way, but operating as the willing steward or servant of the Spirit.

This gets us back to the work of the cross in our life. It must cut away at the flesh and shape us into the image of Christ, which is, as we said before, the reason the Lord must lead us through various spiritual terrains, mountains, valleys, deserts, and flatlands. All are necessary to conform us to the image of Christ (for even He learned obedience through suffering). This is the calling of God on our life, and the Holy Spirit uses all aspects of our life in the body, family, and church to produce what He is after. Not only life but also our experiences in the world. Once we come to Christ, all efforts by God are directed toward reaching His desired ends for our life and the purpose of creation.

The body of Christ is not just a metaphor; it is a spiritual reality. It is the means by which those who are in the family and church are to live collectively as a whole. Just as the physical body has many parts, each with its own task to perform for the health of the whole body, so the body of Christ is composed. Each member has its job to do, all under the direction of the head, which is Christ. It is His will which must be carried out and not the will of any of the diverse parts. When this is accomplished, the life of Christ shines forth. When it is not, division and deformity, even paralysis, are the results.

In the book of Ephesians (5:20–21), just before speaking of the relationships of husband and wife, children and parents, bond servants and masters, Paul prefaces the entire discourse by saying, "Giving thanks always for all things to God the Father in the name of our Lord Jesus Christ, submitting to one another in the fear of God." In the body of Christ, we are called to submit to one another as well as to Christ. Now why is that?

Each part of the body of Christ has its unique function to perform, an operation requiring its particular abilities. An eye is made for seeing, an ear for hearing; the eyes and ears are "gifted" in that way in both the physical and spiritual bodies. So to gain the benefits of what is seen, the ear (and all other parts of body) must submit to the vision of the eye. Likewise, the eye must submit to what is heard by the ear. In that way, the whole body is edified and enjoys perfect health. And of course, all parts must submit to the head. As true believers in Christ, we are indeed called to submission. By this marvelous process, the family and church manifest the living Christ to themselves and the world around them. (More on the call to submission will be discussed later.)

CALLED TO KNOW THE TRUTH

For the Lord is good; His mercy is everlasting, and His truth endures to all generations.

Psalms 100:5

God is Spirit, and those who worship Him must worship in spirit and truth.

John 4:24

And you shall know the truth, and the truth shall make you free.

John 8:32

You are of your father the devil, and the desires of your father you want to do. He was a murderer from the beginning, and does not stand in the truth, because there is no truth in him. When he speaks a lie, he speaks from his own resources, for he is a liar and the father of it.

John 8:44

Jesus said to him, "I am the way, the truth, and the life. No one comes to the Father except through Me."

John 14:6

> However, when He, the Spirit of truth, has come,
> He will guide you into all truth.

John 16:13a

Lies, the distortion of the truth of God, began in the Garden of Eden. Satan seduced Eve by lying, twisting the words of God. And once Adam and Eve were cast from the garden, the entire world system and all of human history were built on lies and half-truths. That is what is meant when we are warned in the Word to love not the world, nor the things of the world (1 John 2:15). John is speaking of the system that Satan and fallen men have created. We have to pass our days *in the world* but are not to be *of the world*, drawn in by its tempting lies and false promises, becoming part of its system.

But praise the Lord, both God's mercy and truth are everlasting! There is no shadow of turning in Him (James 1:17). He is truth itself and has sent His truth in the person of Christ. And coming to know Him sets us free. It is by the Holy Spirit that we come to know Christ, for He is the Spirit of truth who has been sent to guide us into *all* truth, which means coming to know Christ fully. We must come to know Him in all His fullness, far beyond just our personal salvation. That is just the beginning. We must come to see that all of creation and all of scripture point us to Christ (John 5:39), that He is indeed all in all and the sum of all things.

Certainly, while yet in the physical body, our knowledge of Christ will be limited. All of the truth lies yet in eternity. However, we can get to know Him well enough *now* to escape all the chains and dead-ends the lies of Satan have spawned. But the truth (which is Christ) must be learned "in spirit." The Holy Spirit reveals Him to our spirit, which He quickened at our new birth. Before that event, our spirit was as though dead, nonfunctional for all practical purposes. We were confined to the operation of our soul (mind, will, and emotions) even in our understanding of God.

I have written two previous books in which the need of our newborn spirit being separated from our soul is thoroughly explored and discussed. Hebrews 4 tells us that this crucial surgery is accomplished by the Word of God and the work of the cross. Cooperation with the Holy Spirit in this process frees our spirit for the purpose of receiving revelation from the Lord and not mistaking our own thoughts and feelings for those of God. This in turn frees our will to submit to the will of the Lord. When this does not occur, the result is carnality in the name of spirituality and discord and dysfunction in the body and church. When it does come about, the unity and strength of the Spirit are manifested, and the world witnesses a true reflection of Christ.

One critical revelation the Holy Spirit has shown me is that the truth is not something *outside* Christ, areas of truth that He teaches us to follow, but that He, Christ Himself, *is* truth. The difference of these two concepts is immense. For years, I studied, learned, prayed, and at times redoubled my efforts to be *like* Jesus, only to fail over and over again. Then one day, the Holy Spirit opened my eyes to behold a deeper revelation of the glory of Christ: Jesus proclaimed that He is *the* truth, as well as the way and the life, the truth itself. Next, the Spirit began to unfold the true meaning of *all in all* and the *sum of all things* regarding His eternal purpose in His Son.

It is the Father's eternal purpose that everything in all creation be filled with nothing but the life and glory of His Son! And the only possible way for that to become a reality for us, His brothers and sisters, is by an exchanged life, our life for His, which indwells us. Any attempts to simply change our life to become more like Him will fail; only His life released can accomplish the eternal purpose of the Father. So, since those two revelations, I have devoted all my efforts to learn *how* to live by the indwelling life of Christ, knowing that nothing of any spiritual worth lies outside Christ Himself.

(There will be much more on this crucial topic later.)

But for now, I want to assure you, "knowing" this truth has already freed me in so many ways and caused me to both glorify the Lord and enjoy Him more than ever!

CALLED TO PRAY

Likewise the Spirit also helps in our weaknesses. For we do not know what we should pray for as we ought, but the Spirit Himself makes intercession for us with groanings which cannot be uttered. Now He who searches the hearts knows what the mind of the Spirit is, because He makes intercession for the saints according to the will of God.

Romans 8:26–27

You ask and do not receive, because you ask amiss, that you may spend it on your pleasures.

James 4:3

Rejoice always, pray without ceasing, in everything give thanks: for this is the will of God in Christ Jesus for you.

1 Thessalonians 5:16–18

Let us therefore come boldly to the throne of grace, that we may obtain mercy and find grace to help in time of need.

Hebrews 4:16

Who may ascend into the hill of the Lord? Or who may stand in His holy place? He who has clean hands and a pure heart.

Psalms 24:4

Now it came to pass, as He was praying in a certain place, when He ceased, that one of His disciples said to Him. "Lord, teach us to pray, as John also taught his disciples."

Luke 11:1

Be still and know that I am God.

Psalms 46:10

Most of us talk about prayer more than we actually do it. And yet it is one of the most important things we are called to do. For I am convinced that nothing is released from heaven to earth unless somebody prays it forth. God has many things He would like to send our way, but He waits for somebody to pray for it. It is amazing that the creator of all things has limited Himself in this way, and it places a tremendous demand and responsibility on us!

This, of course, means that we must discern the will of God. What does He desire to do in a particular situation? What is the Holy Spirit trying to convey to those who are faithful to pray? Such prayer certainly leaves no room for self-centeredness, which unfortunately forms the bulk of prayers heavenward. Our Father knows we have many needs, and He will answer them, but He longs for us to put *His* needs first. That is why Christ says in Matthew 6:33, "But seek first the kingdom of God and His righteousness, and all these things shall be added to you." Otherwise, we will be guilty of asking amiss, often consuming the blessings sent to us in our own lusts or not receiving at all.

Jesus often went apart from His disciples and everyday activities in order to pray. I believe that much of His time in prayer was spent in silence before the Father, listening for His will, for instructions, and the path He was to take next. These were acts of self-surrender, praising God for His goodness and listening for the still, small voice for comfort and direction. This is a discipline we should all learn and practice: *loving* and *listening,* as one dear saint calls it. It helps us to re-center and can set the tone for the rest of the day. Much of my inspiration for writing, especially poetry, has come during these moments.

We all love the entreaty of Hebrews 5:16 for us to come boldly and confidently to the throne of grace in our time of need. But the Lord has cautioned me to also come humbly, that if we desire to come boldly, we must have "clean hands and a pure heart" (Psalm 24:4). There can be no boldness or confidence if our conscience condemns us. Therefore, before we enter boldly, let us pause outside the holy of holies, submitting to the inspection of the Holy Spirit and ridding ourselves of anything which might hinder our prayer, "having our hearts sprinkled from an evil conscience" as it says in Hebrews 10:22. Then we can enter into the presence of the Lord in full confidence.

While we do need set times to pray and commune with the Lord, we should not confine our prayers to those times. Prayer should become a way of life, an ongoing consciousness, an awareness of God throughout the day, wherever we are and whatever we are doing, always ready to include Him in. Surely that is what 1 Thessalonians 5:16 means when it admonishes us to "pray without ceasing."

We must know that the Spirit of the Lord is with us, indeed *within* us, at all times, ever present to encourage, direct, and teach us, desiring nothing but the Father's best for us in all circumstances. He is to be our constant companion, helpmate and friend, with the express purpose of conforming us to the image of Christ.

This makes praise an integral part of prayer. Though it is often difficult to understand, especially while in the midst of a crisis or tragedy, all things *do* happen for good for those who love the Lord and are the called according to His purpose (Romans 8:28). One day when we stand before the Lord and see things the way He sees them, we will fall on our knees in adoration and praise and cry, "Lord, for me You have done [*all*] things well!" We don't always understand now, but we will then. So in that Spirit, we praise Him now! Often and especially when it is a sacrifice to do so. This kind of praise/prayer is of the highest order, a full surrender to the wisdom and goodness of God.

We often struggle in prayer, not sure what or how to pray; Romans 8:26–27 states the problem quite clearly but then assures us that this should not be a hindrance to true prayer. For within us dwells the Holy Spirit, and it is He whom we must turn to for guidance and empowerment in prayer. The disciples of Jesus had the same difficulty, so in Luke 11:1, they asked the Lord to teach them how to pray. What followed is what has become known as the Lord's Prayer. What Christ gave was to be a *pattern* of true prayer, however, and not a kind of ritual or mantra to be repeated verbatim over and over again.

In my book *From the Garden to the Kingdom*, I devote an entire chapter to this subject, fully aware that whole books have been written on the Lord's answer to the disciples.

But here I would like to give only a brief outline of the Lord's Prayer as a pattern of prayer that is well-pleasing to the Father, the key elements of the prayer.

First of all, the introduction and closing serve as perfect bookends of a perfect prayer: "Our Father in heaven, Hallowed be Your name" and "for Yours is the kingdom and the power and the glory forever" both bow to the glory that is God's alone, honoring His name, recognizing and praising His omnipotence and sovereignty, all creation subject to and dependent upon Him.

The first request the prayer makes is for His kingdom to come, that it might be on earth as it is in heaven once again. Matthew is the gospel of the kingdom, so it is quite natural that a prayer for its coming should appear. The book of John is the new Genesis, bearing a remarkable resemblance to the first book of the Holy Canon, both declaring, "In the beginning…" (Genesis 1:1, John 1:1). But Matthew stresses, "Repent, for the kingdom of heaven is at hand" (Matthew 3:2, 4:17). The Father's eyes have been on the kingdom from the very beginning, and a careful study of the concept of the kingdom reveals that the kingdom is present anywhere and at any time in which Christ truly rules, spiritually in all hearts that have totally surrendered to Christ and have made Him all in all in their lives.

Of course the coming of the kingdom is the last thing Satan wants to happen, so he uses a variety of lies and schemes to prevent its coming. One of those is to cause deprivation of basic needs in the lives of believers. "Give us this day our daily bread" is the Lord's answer to that threat and a guarantee that He will provide our sustenance, even as He did for Elijah when he was fleeing from Jezebel (1 Kings 19). And complete dependence is evident by the words *daily* bread; no need to store up or hoard provisions but instead believe the Lord for each day's needs.

Temptation to sin is another of the devil's devices to cause us to stumble and fall short in our pursuit of the kingdom. So the words "and forgive us our debts (trespasses)" and "and do not lead us into temptation, but deliver us from the evil one" (Matthew 6:12, 13) appear to keep those tempting lies away from us, that we might not sin and have forgiveness for those times in which we do fail. But notice that we are only forgiven *as we forgive others*: unforgiveness binds us, and this part of the prayer can become a curse instead of a blessing if we fail to forgive those who have wronged us.

The Lord's Prayer is a model prayer, a prayer that hits the mark. Reverence, praise, and dependence on the goodness and mercy of God are featured, and prayers for provision and deliverance from sin are also paramount. Praying and living in such a way is the very essence of the kingdom and will hasten its coming!

Much more could be written on the call to pray; again, whole books have been devoted to the subject. The most important point I want to leave you with here is this: pray, pray, pray! Don't just talk about it waiting for a more convenient time or place. Make prayer an integral part of your life. Pray, and see what the Lord will do!

CALLED FROM FAITH TO FAITH

Now faith is the substance of things hoped for, the evidence of things not seen.

Hebrews 11:1

But to think soberly, as God has dealt to each one a measure of faith.

Romans 12:3

So then faith comes by hearing, and hearing by the word of God.

Romans 10:17

For by grace through faith you have been saved, and that not of yourselves; it is the gift of God, not of works, lest anyone should boast.

Ephesians 2:8–9

For assuredly, I say to you, if you have faith as a mustard seed, you will say to this mountain, "Move from here to there," and it will move; and nothing will be impossible for you.

Matthew 17:20

For in it the righteousness of God is revealed from faith to faith; as it is written, "The just shall live by faith."

Romans 1:17

Scripture makes it very clear that our initial faith is a gift of God, that every man has been given a measure of faith. And from that point on, every aspect of God that we gain is through faith; indeed, we are called to go *from* faith *to* faith, from the basic to higher and higher realms of faith. Our initial faith is for the purpose of salvation, but our growth in faith is for bearing fruit. At each level, our current faith is tested so that we might reach greater faith, thereby bearing more fruit unto the Lord. Without such testing, there can be no growth or increase in faith.

Once we have been convinced that the Bible is the Word of God and believe, grace through faith saves us from the righteous judgment of God. For as Romans 1:17 states, "Faith comes by hearing, and hearing by the word of God." And just as it was for Abraham, our faith is counted as righteousness. But of course there is much more to hear from the Word of God (who cannot lie), truth in which to place our belief. That is why it is so important for us to know the Word. For without *hearing* it, how can we believe and obtain the object of faith in that area?

The life of Abraham, who has become known as the father of faith, provides an excellent study of the journey of faith we are all called to walk. It was truly a gift of God when He appeared and told Abraham to leave his home and family and travel to a place He would show him later. Of course, great promises for Abraham's obedience were also given, as is the case when believers are promised eternal and abundant life to leave the world behind to follow Jesus.

It was not long, however, before the testing of Abraham's faith occurred. First came a famine in the land, and Abraham had a choice to make. He chose to go to Egypt where there was no famine. On the surface, this seems quite understandable, but in actuality, it set the stage for Abraham faltering in his trust in God. Egypt in scripture is a picture of the world, the system created by Satan and fallen man from which we are told to flee (2 Corinthians 6:17, Isaiah 52:11). There is very seldom a famine in Egypt; the world takes care of its own. But Egypt is not to be the solution to spiritual problems and our walk of faith.

Once Abraham got to Egypt, his second failure quickly followed; one bad choice often breeds another. In this case, fear, the very opposite of faith, was the cause of Abraham's temporary downfall. He lied and told the pharaoh that Sarah was his sister and not his wife, a sin he was to repeat later as well.

My own personal experience bears witness to all the foregoing: any time I have compromised and made choices that were not motivated by faith and trust in God, I came to regret it. And at times it took me awhile to repent and get back on track, which usually made ample room for more bad choices. That is why the Word tells us that *anything* that is not of faith is sin! (Romans 14:23).

Our faith in the Word of God is often tested by time. He just doesn't seem to answer and fulfill His promise quickly enough. That was certainly the case for Abraham. Many years had passed since the Lord had spoken and promised Abraham a son. He and Sarah must have wondered if they had really heard from the Lord at all or perhaps had misunderstood Him. At any rate, at Sarah's suggestion, Abraham fathered a son by Hagar, Sarah's Egyptian handmaiden (please note: Egypt again!). Of course, Ishmael was not the promised son; he was a child of the flesh, and flesh can never beget spirit (John 3:6).

Most of us have been guilty of this same misstep in our walk with the Lord. We are sure we have heard from Him on a particular issue and proceed on that basis, only to find that time doesn't seem to bear it out. We begin to question our discernment in such matters. And indeed, we may have misheard or misunderstood. Such times can give rise to confusion and lack of trust in future guidance from the Holy Spirit. But I have had many experiences of this sort in which the Word of the Lord did eventually come to pass. The problem was one of time, the delay between promise and fulfillment. This can be a most difficult testing of our faith, but one which we must pass if we are to grow and continue our journey with the Lord.

Abraham was indeed a man of great faith, a true giant in his trust of God. But even he failed along the way! I find that very comforting in my own walk and love that the Bible does not cover up the flaws of even the greatest champions of the faith. We all fall short along the way, but praise God, He is always there to pick us up and, if we are willing, empower us to persevere to the end.

That was certainly what happened to Abraham. In due time, Isaac, the true child of promise, was born. My, how that must have bolstered the faith of both Abraham and Sarah! Twenty-five years after the promise was made, when Abraham was near one hundred years old and Sarah ninety, the Lord came through! And how they must have loved that boy, love which was soon to be tested.

The ultimate test for Abraham came in Genesis 22 when the Lord said, "Take now your son, your only son Isaac, whom you love, and go to the land of Moriah, and offer him there as a burnt offering on one of the mountains of which I shall tell you." (Is it not interesting that in the eyes of the Lord, Isaac was Abraham's *only* son?)

Genesis 22:3 is quite astounding and shows us just how far the faith of Abraham had matured by this point. Without delay, he prepared and took Isaac to be sacrificed! No questioning of the Lord, no second-guessing. Simply obedience! Amazing! It was not until the New Testament, in Hebrews 11, the great faith chapter, that we get an explanation of Abraham's quick response to the command of God:

> By faith Abraham, when he was tested, offered up Isaac, and he who had received the promises offered up his only begotten son, of whom it was said, 'In Isaac your seed shall be called,' concluding that God was able to raise him up, even from the dead, from which he also received him in a figurative sense.
>
> Hebrews 11:17–19

There was no way for all nations to be blessed through the seed of Abraham and Isaac if Isaac was to die. So if he did die, God would surely raise him from the dead in order to fulfill His promise, Abraham reasoned. What faith, what trust! This is where we all must go if we are to become true men and women of faith. Whatever it is that we love most, we must be willing to sacrifice at a moment's notice if the Lord so desires. For this is the essence of going *from* faith *to* faith, of fully trusting in the Lord no matter what.

Early in my walk of faith with the Lord, He expanded my understanding and confidence in the gift of healing. I had been raised in a church that believed that the gifts of the Spirit had ceased after the death of the apostles, which included the gift of healing. So the Lord decided to show me otherwise. I was part of a prayer and meditation group in which we studied a book called *A Search for God.* After our study was concluded for the evening, we would dim the lights and pray. As I was quietly meditating on the work of Christ and the cross, I suddenly received a strong impression to go pray for a woman who was part of the group. She wore a hearing aid and had had several operations through the years in an effort to restore her hearing, all to no avail.

At first I tried to ignore the thoughts, but even as I did, they grew stronger and stronger. Then quite suddenly, my hands became extremely warm. I quit fighting the suggestion, and when the lights were turned back on, I walked over, placed my hands on the woman's ears, and prayed silently and very briefly. From that moment on, the young woman could hear perfectly! I was amazed to say the least. But my newfound enthusiasm became quite dashed in the days that followed.

Thanking the Lord for the gift of healing, I set out to pray for any sickness and affliction that came my way. As you might expect, the results were mixed: some people recovered, other did not. Some even died. I became very disappointed and confused. I searched the scriptures and prayed for some explanation but found nothing to satisfy my doubts and consternation. I finally decided to put the problem to rest, knowing that God can and does heal. I still pray for the sick and have seen many miracles. But once I pray or lay on hands or anoint with oil (or whatever the

Spirit leads me to do), I leave it in the Lord's hands, for it is His sovereignty that decides all things. I pray and then rest in that, praising Him whether healing comes or not.

I still have a long way to go in my own walk of faith. There are deeper domains of faith than I have yet experienced. And I am sure that the same is true for you. How else can we explain the Lord's own words in Matthew 17:20 when Christ said, "If you have faith as a mustard seed…nothing will be impossible for you."? And when He told us in John 14:12 that we would be able to do what He did, and even greater things, because He was going to the Father? Those are indeed words I have heard and believe, so, Lord, increase my faith in those areas where I am still deficient in my belief. And increase the faith of my brothers and sisters, Lord, all those who make up Your marvelous body! Amen

CALLED TO MAKE DISCIPLES

And Jesus came and spoke to them, saying, "All authority has been given to Me in heaven and on earth. Go therefore and make disciples of all nations, baptizing them in the name of the Father and of the Son and of the Holy Spirit, teaching them to observe all things that I have commanded you; and lo, I am with you always, even to the end of the age."

Matthew 28:18–20

Then Jesus said to those Jews who believed Him, "If you abide in My word, you are My disciples indeed. And you shall know the truth, and the truth shall make you free."

John 8:31–32

If anyone comes to Me and does not hate his father and mother, wife and children, brothers and sisters, yes, and his own life also, he cannot be My disciple.

Luke 14:26

So likewise, whoever of you does not forsake all that he has cannot be My disciple.

Luke 14:33

And he brought them out and said, "Sirs, what must I do to be saved?" So they said, "Believe on the Lord Jesus Christ, and you shall be saved, you and your household."

Acts 16:30–31

But what does it say? "The word is near you, in your mouth and in your heart" (that is, the word of faith which we preach): that if you confess with your mouth the Lord Jesus and believe in your heart that God has raised Him from the dead, you will be saved.

Romans 10:8–9

Just before ascending into heaven after His resurrection, Jesus spoke to His disciples and gave them what has become known as the Great Commission: to go into all the world and make disciples of all nations, baptizing them in the name of the Triune God and teaching them to observe all things that He had commanded them. He assured them that all authority in heaven and on earth had been given to Him and that He would be with them always. We also know from Luke 10:19 that He had already given the apostles that same authority: "Behold, I give you the authority to trample on serpents and scorpions, and over all the power of the enemy, and nothing by any means shall hurt you."

That commission given to the apostles is now ours, the task of all born-again disciples to reproduce our own kind, and the same authority to do so has been given to us. We are in Christ, and He resides in us, so we are more than well armed for the task! Our first question, however, should be, *what is a disciple?* Are all believers disciples? Is there any distinction between the two? The Word declares that there is.

We know from Ephesians 2:8–10 that we are saved by grace through faith alone; salvation is a free gift from God appropriated by faith. That is the requirement to be a believer, and such a person will escape the great white throne judgment of God and spend eternity in heaven. But to be a disciple requires much more: such a believer must deny himself, forsake all things for the sake of Christ, and be willing to take up his cross daily and follow Christ. He cannot put his love of family or anything else above his love for Christ.

If we read the commission more closely, we notice that the apostles were to teach potential disciples *all* Christ had *commanded* them, to *observe* those commandments. So from these words, we see that to be a disciple, we must *do* many things. This is very similar to going from faith to faith, previously discussed: initial faith unto salvation is a free gift of God, but maturing in faith requires being tested and overcoming obstacles the enemy puts in our way to prevent further progress. The same is true if we are to pass from being a believer to becoming a disciple.

First of all, the Lord had taught the apostles many things, all the deeper truths of walking in the Spirit and becoming an overcomer (Revelations 2 and 3). Those who are to teach these truths need to have learned and experienced the depths of such truths themselves. For like begets like. Obviously, it is the Holy Spirit who does the work in each believer, but in the case of "making" disciples, the Spirit works in and through individuals who are already disciples themselves. Otherwise, such efforts are reduced to fruitless academic teachings of methods and steps.

A true disciple of Christ is dangerous to the kingdom of darkness, so Satan uses all of his lies and wiles to prevent such progress in the life of a believer. Any time a believer strives for a deeper commitment to Christ, our foe throws up all sorts of obstacles in the way. Temptations to sin may become ever more subtle. Division in the family or church may spring up. A spirit of complacency often must be overcome. In each case, a deeper desire for more of the Lord and greater faith is called for. But many believers simply give in and settle for less, just as all but two of those who left Egypt under Moses never made it to the Promised Land but died in the wilderness along the way.

When Christ beckoned believers to "follow Him," He meant to live the same life of devotion to God that He lived. He learned obedience through the things He suffered, so to follow Him involves our suffering as well. For He said a disciple is not greater than his master, and if the world hated Him, it would also hate us. He also cautioned us to count the cost before deciding to follow Him. In the end, it costs us everything the flesh holds dear. *That* gospel is seldom preached. Most of us in modern-day America have heard a sugarcoated gospel, one designed to attract. But Christ Himself warned against such an understanding of His message. He declared that if we are disciples of His, we will suffer tribulation. Of course, this is followed by His encouragement to be of good cheer, for He has overcome the world system that is bent on enmity against Him and His followers (John 16:33).

To become a true disciple of Christ requires undergoing spiritual surgery, the sword of the Spirit, the Word of God, dividing soul from spirit. Hebrews 4:12 is one of the most important verses in the Bible; everything truly spiritual hinges on it. When Jesus said we must lose our life (fallen soul-life, *psuche*) to find our new life (in which the soul serves our spirit as it receives the guidance of the Holy Spirit and the indwelling life of Christ), He was speaking of this very operation. Our born-again spirit must have control of our life if we are to go from faith to faith and become a disciple of Christ. (I have written two other books, *From the Garden to the Kingdom* and *Pilgrimage,* in which this process is thoroughly explored. For now, I simply mention it again, with the hope that the revelation of the Holy Spirit will open up the critical importance of it for you.)

CALLED TO GIVE

This is My commandment, that you love one another as I have loved you.

John 15:12

So let each one give as he purposes in his heart, not grudgingly or of necessity; for God loves a cheerful giver.

2 Corinthians 9:7

And the King will answer and say to them, "Assuredly, I say to you, inasmuch as you did it to one of the least of these My brethren, You did it to Me."

Matthew 25:40

No one can serve two masters; for either he will hate the one and love the other, or else he will be loyal to the one and despise the other. You cannot serve God and mammon.

Matthew 6:24

Bear one another's burdens, and so fulfill the law of Christ.

Galatians 6:2

Pure and undefiled religion before God and the Father is this: to visit orphans and widows in their trouble, and to keep oneself unspotted from the world.

James 1:27

Give me neither poverty nor riches—Feed me with the food allotted to me; lest I be full and deny You, And say, "Who is the Lord?" Or lest I be poor and steal, and profane the name of my God.

Proverbs 30:8–9

So much could be written on the virtue of giving, for giving is the very nature of our God. Inherent in His great love is grace, giving whether it is deserved or not. The scriptures are full of references to giving (well over two thousand!). I have chosen the few above to illustrate three distinct areas of giving: the giving of our means, the giving of our time, and the giving of grace to others.

Most of us think of giving in terms of money and goods. Indeed, the Bible is full of passages about money and its use and misuse. Monetary value placed upon all things is part of the world system created by Satan and fallen men. With God, all is by grace (Revelations 22:17). When we touch money, we touch the enemy, so we must be careful in how we handle it, holding it lightly, willing to let it go at a moment's notice if God so desires. Certainly, as the old saying goes, it is money that makes the world go around. We must have enough to provide our daily needs, but we must be vigilant that we never allow it to have us!

That was certainly the rich young ruler's problem in Luke 18:18–25: he simply could not let it go. Money and the things it bought had become more important to him than anything else in the world, even his eternal salvation apparently! He chose mammon over God, completely contrary to the words of the Savior (Matthew 6:24). Money can feed the flesh to the point of addiction just as surely as any drug.

When it comes to the giving of money to God, there is much controversy. How much should we give? Is the tithe still binding? If I give freely, will even more come back to me? The New Testament has very little to say on a strict adherence to tithing. But if a faithful Jew was required by law to give at least ten percent of his income (far more than that if you count free-will offerings, etc.), how can we decide under grace and salvation to give less? What I have found in my own experience and in the lives of those I have pastored over the years is this: if a man's heartstrings have truly been touched by Christ, there will be no trouble with his purse-strings. God has given us everything! How can we withhold anything from Him? I like the words of 2 Corinthians 9:7 when it comes to how much I give: "So let each one give as he purposes in his heart, not grudgingly or of necessity; for God loves a cheerful giver."

As far as giving-to-get, the message of prosperity preachers, which has become so widespread in the past few decades, there is something inherently wrong in such motives, and such an idea is completely unwarranted by scripture. Certainly, the Lord will bless generosity, but this should never be our motive for giving. Instead, we should follow the command of Christ in Matthew 6:3, not letting our left hand know what our right hand is doing, neither calling attention to our generosity nor expecting something in return.

The Lord will always take care of His own. The wisdom of Agur in Proverbs 30: 8–9 seems a very good path to follow: to desire neither riches nor poverty but the amount the Lord has allotted for each. For it is He who knows just how much each of us can handle and not be corrupted by it. Such a life is truly blessed, enough to live but not enough to forget God, the hand from which it came.

Early in my Christian walk, I had two very interesting incidents regarding money. Our young family of six was getting by financially, albeit meagerly; there was always enough but just barely. We had just opened our new school, which had taken all the money we had, and enrollment was a few less children than we needed to make ends meet. Christmas was approaching, and we grew concerned. There would simply be no extra money to buy gifts for our four children, ages one, three, four, and six years. The last day before holiday vacation, the secretary of the church building we were renting caught me as we were getting ready to leave for the day.

"Someone left this here for you," she said and handed me a white blank envelope. I opened it and inside was a hundred-dollar bill! I was astonished. When I asked her who it was, she replied she didn't know, that she had never seen the man before. We still don't know who it was, but that was our children's Christmas that year.

We attended church regularly at the time and gave at least one-tenth of what we earned, as well as sharing with others who needed help. We did so willingly and cheerfully, never truly worrying about any lack of basic necessities. Did we receive our anonymous gift for that reason? I don't believe so, not in any one-to-one, cause-and-effect sort of way. We were faithful as best we knew how to be at the time. We had a need, and the Lord met it. In fact, He has continued to do so throughout our married life of forty-two years, in our family affairs as well as the continued success of our school.

The second story is even more pointed. I had just begun preaching, and the organization with which I was associated was having its annual convention. An elderly lady in our congregation invited me to go, saying it was such a glorious event every year. Again, there was not any extra money at the time, but I agreed to go. She drove, so I was spared that expense. It was an all-day affair, so I knew I would need lunch money. I had two one-dollar bills, thinking that would have to do (a snack would suffice until I got home).

Before the main meeting of the day, a missionary spoke. As I listened, I was so moved that it brought tears to my eyes. The collection plate was passed after her talk, and as it came past my row, I put in a dollar. A second plate came down the other row, and as it passed, the Lord reminded me that I had another dollar. So without giving it a moment's thought, I deposited my other dollar in that plate.

Lunchtime came, and I didn't go hungry after all. The elderly lady who had invited me insisted on buying my meal. After lunch, there was a large gathering of people in an auditorium. It was time to get to know each other; I certainly didn't know anyone else there. While I was visiting with other pastors and church members from various churches, a woman approached and tapped me on the shoulder. I didn't know her, and she didn't introduce herself. Instead, she simply said, "The Lord told me to give this to you," and she handed me two twenty-dollar bills!

Now an experience like that could have easily persuaded me to believe the prosperity message—I mean, a quick twenty-to-one return! But I did not take it that way. I believe the Lord impressed upon the woman that I was a young man in need, and she responded in faith and generosity, the same as I had just given to the devoted and faithful missionary. The money was certainly much needed, and I thanked both the Lord and the woman for their faithfulness and generosity.

When it comes to giving our money and goods, I would strongly advise to always ask the Lord what to give monetarily and to always be willing to share food, clothes, etc., to anyone in need that He puts in our path. That is what my wife and I have done, and the Lord has always provided enough for us and for others.

For many, it is much easier to write a check or reach for their wallet than it is to give the gift of their time. But time is a valuable commodity and often means far more than financial assistance. Whether it is spending time with a sick friend, visiting someone in prison, or going to see perfect strangers in a nursing home, time spent with others at the expense of our own is a marvelous gift. After all, we can always make more money, but time is the one thing we can't get back once it is spent.

James said that pure religion is visiting orphans and widows in their troubles (James 1:27). Certainly, if we are able to ease those troubles with money or goods, we should do so. But it is the visiting, taking the time to care, that matters most. During my trips to nursing homes, so many of the elderly just needed someone to sit and listen to them, to trade stories, to laugh, to sing, and to pray. Some had no one else who came to see them, not even relatives.

A dear old saint in our church who has gone on to her reward was a beautiful example of the mutual benefits of taking time for one another. She had been a shut-in for some time, quite old and unable to attend church, so I would go see her as often as I could. I think we both looked forward to those times of fellowship. I would go thinking I would cheer her up, and I was always successful. But in the end, I think I was more energized and encouraged by our time together than she was! She had such joy and faith that always bubbled to the surface. We would laugh, cry, pray, and sing for much longer than I had planned to stay, and I would always leave feeling exuberant and more excited about the Lord than when I arrived. I miss those times and look forward to reuniting in heaven. Thank you, Nellie!

Although ever-expanding advances in technology have afforded us many benefits undreamed of only a few years ago, some detrimental effects have also accompanied such progress. Rather than mentioning them all, let's take a look at human relationships and taking time for one another. More and more people, starting from a very young age, are spending more and more time on machines (computers, smartphones, high-tech games, etc.) and less and less quality time with one another. Everywhere you go, everyone seems to be calling, texting, gaming, or checking messages. Some children bury themselves in these activities several hours a day; they hardly look up to say hello when you come to visit.

I am an educator and have noticed some very negative effects on the learning process in children during this high-tech age: shorter attention spans, a complete dependence on technology, less ability in the area of critical thinking, and certainly less and less time spent reading, to mention a few.

But of even more concern is the inability to interact with one another in positive ways, seemingly not understanding what is socially acceptable and what is not. Of course, they have an app for that too! (I could hardly believe it when I saw this being advertised.) There is simply no substitute for flesh-and-blood interrelationships; this is one of the key aspects and needs that make us human.

Jesus seemed to have taken time for everyone, and He is ever our example in all things. He would wander about and interact with all sorts of people. He gave them His full attention, never seeming to be in a hurry and ministered to them in whatever way they needed, whether it was encouragement, healing, or even a word of rebuke. So let us examine our own day-to-day lives and evaluate ourselves in our actual giving the gift of time to others. Let's make adjustments if we see we fall short in this critical area. Let us not remain in the category that in spite of more and more "time-saving" devices, we still do not use that time saved as a gift to others. Our lives and the lives of others will be enriched by such a change.

Jesus's commandment in John 15:12 that we are to love one another as He loves us is so far-reaching in its implications. For within His love given to us are all the other graces (forgiveness, mercy, long-suffering, forbearance, humility, etc.). For this reason, I consider the giving of grace the greatest gift of all. And yet, ironically, among true believers in Christ, the gift of grace is often sadly missing. A believer should be quite difficult to offend, and yet, as one saint said in his blog, Christians are the easiest people in the world to offend, especially when it comes to differences in the understanding of faith and doctrine.

As a result, the church has suffered greatly in the areas of unity and tolerance. In such a scenario, internal division and a poor witness to the unbelieving world have resulted, leading many to have a false idea of what Christ and true Christianity is all about. The only one who profits in such a situation is Satan; indeed, discord and a divided body of Christ has been one of his chief tactics and assaults on the church.

This ought not to be. Of course, I am not advocating tolerance to the point of agreement with some other gospel. We must reject all unbiblical or extra-biblical teaching, but even this must be done with grace. After all, how can we help anyone to a better understanding of biblical truth if we are condescending or even malicious in our rejection? We should follow the example of Priscilla and Aquila in Acts 18 when they took Apollos aside and imparted to him a more accurate understanding of the way of God (v. 24–26).

Apollos was an eloquent speaker and mighty in the scriptures, and yet I have no doubt that he gladly received the words of Priscilla and Aquila, largely due to the way they corrected him. And Apollos was teachable, which is a trait we should all retain throughout our walk with the Lord. We should not, however, automatically accept any new word that we hear; rather, be like the Bereans (Acts 17:10–11) who always searched the scriptures to see if what they heard could be verified by the Word of God.

Of course, this requires that we be men and women of the Word, as it says in 2 Timothy 2:15, "rightly dividing the word of truth." For if we do not have a firm grasp of spiritual truth, it lays us open to all sort of false teaching and insidious inroads made by the enemy. In recent years, it has become quite common and popular to give personal experience precedence over clear scriptural teaching to the contrary. This should never be: the Word and the Spirit should always be in agreement with each other. When they are not, a supposed personal word from the Spirit should be seriously questioned if not completely rejected. We must subject all spiritual understanding to the test of Scripture.

Returning to giving the gift of grace to all, as Christ would have us to live, let us use the story of Corrie ten Boom to make a crucial point. Perhaps you are familiar with her story. Corrie and her family were not Jewish but decided to hide Jews from the Nazis during World War II. Eventually they were found out and were sent to a German concentration camp. Corrie's parents and sister did not survive the horrible ordeal, but Corrie did.

After the war, she realized that in spite of her tragic loss, Christ would have her forgive her captors. She thought she had done so, and even traveled and gave talks on her experience, always highlighting the importance of forgiveness. At the end of one such meeting, as the audience was breaking up and being dismissed, she looked up to see a familiar face coming forward to meet her. The middle-aged man had obviously been weeping. As he got closer, Corrie suddenly recognized him: it was the prison guard who had been so cruel during the family's stay in the concentration camp, the chief tormentor you might say!

Suddenly all her talk about forgiveness came tumbling down! As the man was almost up to the stage, Corrie cried out to the Lord, "I can't do this, Jesus!" But then an amazing thing happened: as she knew that *she* could not forgive the former Nazi, the life of Christ came forth and forgave him through Corrie! When the man reached her, weeping aloud, Corrie embraced him and spoke the words of genuine forgiveness. Through this marvelous experience, Corrie realized that all her former talks about forgiveness, no matter the situation, may or may not have been the real thing. After that, she learned to depend on the life of Christ being released and not upon her own strength and words. I believe this forever changed the life of this wonderful woman of God.

And it should change ours as well. The only way for us to love as Jesus loved is to allow His Life to be released and express itself. It is never a matter of trying harder and harder to be *like* Jesus, but a matter of His indwelling Life and will coming forth. Anything else will be but a man-made lookalike, and we may discover, as did Corrie ten Boom, that the Lord will arrange circumstances with a challenge to our own efforts that is impossible to meet. Such an experience is actually both good and liberating. Only Christ has perfectly overcome the flesh and completely defeated Satan. He alone has all the power and all the glory and is indeed all in all and the sum of all things!

As a disciple of Christ, the call to give is a command, not a request—to give of our means and goods and our time and to extend the grace of God to all. For the Lord's commandment for us to love as He has loved us carries with it the call to give, to esteem others more highly than ourselves, in fact, to lose our soul of self-centeredness altogether to gain our true soul, one that will always submit itself to the will of Christ.

THE CALL TO A NEW CREATION

Therefore from now on, we regard no one according to the flesh. Even though we have known Christ according to the flesh, yet now we know Him thus no longer. Therefore, if anyone is in Christ, he is a new creation; old things have passed away; behold, all things have become new.

2 Corinthians 5:16–17

I beseech you therefore, brethren, by the mercies of God, that you present your bodies a living sacrifice, holy, acceptable to God, which is your reasonable service. And do not be conformed to this world, but be transformed by the renewing of your mind, that you may prove what is that good and acceptable and perfect will of God.

Romans 12:1–2

I will give you a new heart and put a new spirit within you.

Ezekiel 36:26a

He who finds his life will lose it, and he who loses his life for My sake will find it.

Matthew 10:39

In order to understand the new creation we have become in Christ Jesus, we must first better understand the old creation. Before original sin, the creation of man was not complete, and after that first transgression (before the coming of Christ), man remained in an incomplete state so far as God's original plan. Adam and Eve, prior to sin, lived in a state of innocence: the concept of good and evil was not yet part of their consciousness. They communed with God, Spirit to spirit, in unbroken fellowship and worship. But there was still a choice to be made to complete their creation: the choice between God and themselves.

Listening to the serpent, they were seduced to choose self over God. When that happened, they underwent what we commonly call the fall: their spirit became as though dead, nonfunctional, and their soul (*psuche*—mind, will, and emotions) ascended to the seat of control in their lives. *They* could decide good from evil, independent of God. As a result, they were cast from the garden (the presence of God) and became wanderers upon the earth, cut off from direct communication with their Maker, with a death sentence upon their lives.

Such was the condition of all men until Christ, and such are all men without Christ today. In very short summary, this is the old creation.

It took Christ coming in the flesh, as a man, to reverse the curse, complete the creation of man, and make a way back to God. He is indeed the second Adam, the Glorious One who succeeded in all the ways Adam and Eve failed. He overcame sin, death, and Satan, His resurrection and ascension the proof of His transcendent victory! All those who repent and believe in His atoning death escape judgment and eternal separation from God. They are given both a new heart and a new spirit, enabled once again to directly commune with God.

Not only are true believers in Christ saved from condemnation and judgment, but the Spirit of Christ baptizes, fills, and indwells their new spirit! Christ has come to live inside! This too is needed for the completion of the creation of man. For while we are yet in the flesh, the battle goes on, with Satan doing all he can to stir up the flesh, and the Holy Spirit ever ready to arm us with our spiritual weapons in Christ to defeat the enemy and breathe more life into the new creation. The process will not be completed until the return of Christ and we receive our glorified body (like unto His!).

Then man will finally be as the Father intended, the dominion he was given in Genesis 1:26–28 his again, dominion over all things, including Satan and all demonic forces the enemy can bring to bear. In his transformed state (the new creation complete), the redeemed will rule and reign with Christ for a thousand years upon the earth and then in the new heaven and new earth forever.

In short summary, *this* is the new creation referred to by Paul in 2 Corinthians 5:16–17. Hallelujah! What a salvation and what a Savior!

At this point though, it seems important and necessary to speak at length on the battle all believers, after their redemption, must face. While we are yet in the flesh, Satan will continue his attacks and deceptions, the flesh against the spirit and spirit against the flesh. In many ways, this battle is unnecessary. For God did not intend for our flesh to do battle with Satan, for there is no way for the flesh (including its will, mind, and emotions) to win in such a struggle. It is not a matter of the old man being reformed and becoming more and more like Christ. Such a thing is impossible.

For that reason, God arranged for the old man's death! In Romans 6:6, we are told quite clearly by Paul that our old man was crucified with Christ. And since this is a fact, Paul admonishes us in 6:11 of Romans, "Likewise you also, reckon yourselves to be dead indeed to sin, but alive to God in Christ Jesus our Lord." This is the Word of God on the old man! Our job is in the "reckoning" or appropriating by faith this marvelous fact.

Of course, such a fact seems impossible to the rational mind: *I wasn't even alive when Christ died on the cross, so how in the world could I have ever been crucified with Him?* I wrestled with this dilemma for some time myself. But then the Lord opened my eyes to the equally astonishing fact that all who are His have been *in Christ* (Ephesians 1:3–4 and elsewhere) from before the foundation of the world. With this came the realization that God is not limited to time and space. He has been able to see all and do all from eternity past to eternity future! Once I understood and believed that, it was quite simple to see how I am "in Christ," for He placed me there long, long ago. And once I was put there, nothing could take me out (Romans 8:35–39). Therefore, where He has been, I have been, and where He is, I am! Granted, these are spiritual facts and must become real to us by faith in the Word of God, but then, so do *all* the things that are ours in Christ. Again, all I can say is *hallelujah*!

So you can see that the battle with Satan after salvation in some ways ought not to be, right? But our enemy uses ever more subtle ways of deception to revive and stir up the flesh. There seems to be residues of our old life to which he can still appeal, even after the belief and reckoning of Romans 6:6 and 6:11. The apostle Paul struggled with this apparent contradiction himself. Romans 7 details his fight with the remaining flesh of the old man—this *after* he realized and declared the old man dead in Romans 6!

But praise the Lord, the Holy Spirit showed him (and us!) the way out of the dilemma. For Romans 8 gives the answer: "There is therefore now no condemnation to those who are in Christ Jesus, who do not walk according to the flesh, but according to the Spirit. For [*the law of the Spirit of Life in Christ Jesus has made me free from the law of sin and death*]" (Romans 8:1–2). The old law of sin and death has been overcome by a higher law, the law of the Spirit of Life in Christ Jesus! We are no longer under the old law; that is, unless we allow ourselves, by being drawn back by Satan, to try to defeat him through willpower and our own strength. This is a battle that cannot be won and leads to frustration and confusion.

What must be remembered is that this new law, the law of the Spirit of Life, is *in* Christ Jesus, who is *in* us. So for it to operate, our will must be surrendered to His will, rather than trying to defeat the enemy with our own power. By submitting our will to His will, the indwelling Life of Christ is released, and the law of the Spirit of Life easily overcomes the law of sin and death, just as surely as Christ has already overcome Satan. This is the only way for us to overcome the power of sin while yet in this body of flesh. Once again, praise His holy name, for He has not only saved us from the penalty of sin but also freed us from its power as well!

The other important fact to recall is that we are not alone. One on one against Satan is not the Lord's way.

For that reason, He has placed us in His body with other believers and Himself as head. As discussed in a previous chapter, not one part of the body can do all the work of the body; all of its members are needed. By submitting to one another and to our head, even Christ, there is no way for Satan to defeat us. That is the reason Satan works so hard to divide the body, to weaken it as a whole, and to separate and "pick off" individual members who stray away. Never forget how much we need one another! And do all you can to maintain the unity of the body (Ephesians 4:1–3).

How glorious is the new creation to which the Spirit has called us! We are given a new heart and new spirit so that we can commune with God the Father and God the Son through the Spirit of God. We have been baptized, filled, and indwelt by the Holy Spirit and Christ to guide and empower us against all the assaults, deceptions, and temptations of the enemy. And being part of the body of Christ, when properly functioning, cannot be defeated by anything in heaven or earth! And last but not least, we await the return of our Lord and Savior, Jesus Christ, at which time we will be clothed with our glorified body and finally be the finished product ordained by the Trinity before the foundation of the world. And then, of course, ruling and reigning with Christ during the millennium, and then forever and ever in the new heaven and new earth! Who could say no to such a calling? Glorifying God and enjoying Him forever? What do you think!?

CALLED TO SUBMISSION

For its full development, the new creation requires submission. But to the flesh, especially to the soul, *submission* is a much hated word and concept. The opposite of submission is rebellion, the very sin of Adam and Eve in the Garden of Eden. And the end of rebellion is to be in control oneself, exactly what occurred after mankind's original transgression. To be as god themselves, independent of the Creator, was the great temptation Adam and Eve could not resist. So they were cast from the presence of God, their spirit becoming nonfunctional and their soul (mind, will, and emotions) ascending to the throne of their life—their existence controlled by what they thought, felt, and decided. Such was our life before coming to Christ, and it continues to be a problem for most new believers in Christ.

The forbidden fruit from the tree of the knowledge of good and evil has had a deep and drastic effect on humankind, one that persists long after the experience of salvation. Men are so accustomed to being in charge of their own lives that most continue to do so even after coming to Christ: of course, they set out to do "good" instead of the sins they committed before salvation, but they unwittingly do so by their own will and strength. This eventually leads to failure and frustration.

The reactions to this roadblock vary: Some dig in and try even harder, making new resolutions and efforts, only to fail again. Others resign themselves to falling short and live lukewarm Christian lives. Some actually give up and return to a life of sin. But for those who continue to seek God, praying and staying in the Word, the answer comes—submission. They learn that even Jesus did not live by His own mind, will, and strength, but by the will and power of the Father through the Holy Spirit. He chose not to live the life of His own soul, saying that without the Father, He could do nothing. And in another place, He told us that without Him, we can do nothing.

I can't do this is such a critical revelation! And of course, its corollary follows: *Christ has and can!* It is His Life within that must be released for victory to come, and that release depends on submission (not *my* will but *Yours*, Lord*)*. Each time we do this, we have left the tree of death and eaten from the tree of life!

The benefits of living in the body, family, church submitted to Christ, and one another are indeed incredible (once again, at a loss for words to adequately describe!). First of all, being drawn and accepted by the unconditional love of God has profound effects. Separation and isolation, even a sense of alienation, has been the lot of all men since Adam and Eve were cast from the garden and the presence of God. All human relationships were damaged.

Even man and wife, the intimate male-female relationship, was deeply wounded. Part of the curse of sin was a conflict between man and woman, which has become known as the battle of the sexes, for the Lord God said to the woman, "Your desire shall be for you husband, and he shall rule over you" (Genesis 3:15). What God had intended to be a coregency had become a struggle for dominance. In the body of Christ, this has been healed, man and woman once again equal partners, each with a different function within the body and family but equal and integral parts.

> Husbands, love your wives, just as Christ also loved the church and gave Himself for her…This is a great mystery, but I speak concerning Christ and the church.
>
> Ephesians 5: 25, 32

What a thought to digest! Naturally, loving our wives as Christ loved the church is impossible. Only the indwelling Life of Christ being released can achieve such a feat. And all other relationships are healed as well by that same process of submission and release.

The unconditional love of God, perfect love itself, casts out all fear, fear being another of many reasons that man struggles with submission. First John 4:17–18 confirms this: "Love has been perfected among us in this: that we may have boldness in the day of judgment; because as He is, so we are in this world. There is no fear in love, but perfect love casts out fear, because fear involves torment. But he who fears has not been made perfect in love."

The opposite of faith is fear, which man has had upon him since original sin and alienation from God. Death and the fear of death have loomed over him. But the love of God has dispelled this and all other fear, for the "just shall live by faith" (Habakkuk 2:4, Romans 1:17). True faith and the love of Christ banish fear, which is a key obstacle to the call to submission.

Pride and independence are also deterrents to submission. Living in the freedom and independence of

America has greatly fostered and enhanced these two traits. We are taught early on, both at home and in school, to be self-sufficient, which, for making our way in a fallen world, can be beneficial and even necessary. But such a teaching has a double edge to it: it feeds the very things that caused man to fall in the first place! But little by little, by the love of Christ and the illumination of the Word by the Holy Spirit (plus the repeated failures of our carnal attempts to be spiritual!), pride and independence are laid aside.

Once we belong to the body and family of God, we learn our true identity. By losing our false identity (our soul before coming to Christ), we gain our true self, the one created in the image and likeness of God, the one who is to be a servant or steward of the Holy Spirit via our spirit. Once our spirit is awakened and is enabled to receive revelation from the Holy Spirit, reestablishing the order of control in our life, spirit, soul, and body, the completion of our creation as God originally intended is well on its way. Growing in grace and cooperation with the Holy Spirit completes the process.

Being part of the body and family of God insures our support by other members. Ephesians 2:19–22 says, "Now, therefore, you are no longer strangers and foreigners, but fellow citizens with the saints and members of the household of God, having been built on the foundation of the apostles and prophets, Jesus Christ Himself being the chief cornerstone, in whom the whole building, being fitted together, grows into a holy temple in the Lord, in whom you also are built together for a dwelling place of God in the Spirit."

So long as Christ is the chief cornerstone and the foundation is right, we all become what Peter calls lively or living stones in the temple of God, perfectly fitted to

Christ and one another, for the purpose of edification and support. Any other structure will not long endure, nor will it survive the test by fire at the judgment seat of Christ (1 Corinthians 3:11–15). But unity and the true life of the body of Christ require submission, first to Christ and then to one another.

In the body, family, and church, we discover our unique value. Each member has received a special gift or talent that is to be in submission to the Holy Spirit and used to edify one another, which in turn allows the Life of Christ to manifest to a lost and dying world (Romans 12:4–21). If a brother or sister has a gift that I do not possess, and I submit to the operation of their gift, I receive all the benefits of that gift the same as if it were mine (and so do all the other members of the body!). In this way, the body and family are continually refreshed and edified, and Christ can be witnessed by the world.

In God's flock (another way of describing His body, family, and church), we are protected and cared for by the Shepherd Himself as well as by one another. In other words, there is strength and safety in the flock:

> Shepherd the flock of God which is among you, serving as overseers, not by compulsion but willingly, not for dishonest gain but eagerly; nor as being lords over those entrusted to you, but being examples to the flock; and when the Chief Shepherd appears, you will receive the crown of glory that does not fade away. Likewise you younger people, submit yourselves to your elders. Yes, all of you be submissive to one another, and be clothed with humility.
>
> 1 Peter 5:2–5

Bear one another's burdens, and so fulfill the law of
Christ.

Galatians 6:2

Therefore comfort each other and edify one another,
just as you also are doing.

1 Thessalonians 5:11

Praise the Lord!

One other important benefit of being a vital
member of Christ's body, family, and church is that
it allows us to be productive, to accomplish the very
things for which we were created. To drive this
point home, Christ used the picture of a vine and
its branches bearing fruit. In John 15:1–5, He says,

I am the true vine, and My Father is the vinedresser.
Every branch in Me that does not bear fruit He
takes away; and every branch that bears fruit He
prunes, that it may bear more fruit. You are already
clean because of the word which I have spoken to
you. Abide in Me, and I in you. As a branch cannot
bear fruit of itself, unless it abides in the vine,
neither can you, unless you abide in Me. I am the
vine, and you are the branches. He who abides in
Me, and I in him, bears much fruit; for without Me
you can do nothing.

What a beautiful and perfect description of a healthy,
fully submitted body of believers!

CALLED TO BE CONFORMED

I beseech you, therefore, brethren, by the mercies of God, that you present your bodies a living sacrifice, holy, acceptable to God, which is your reasonable service. And do not be conformed to this world, but be transformed by the renewing of your mind, that you may prove what is that good and acceptable and perfect will of God.

Romans 12:1–2

But reject profane and old wives' fables, and exercise yourselves toward godliness. For bodily exercise profits a little, but godliness is profitable for all things, having promise of the life that now is and that which is to come.

Timothy 4:7–8

For whom He foreknew, He also predestined to be conformed to the image of His Son, that He might be the firstborn among many brethren.

Romans 8:29

My little children, for whom I labor in birth again until Christ is formed in you.

Galatians 4:19

To be like Jesus should be our greatest desire and hope; the Word calls it to be *conformed to His image*. But just how does that come about? How is such a marvelous transformation even possible? We always think in terms of what we must *do* to achieve a particular goal or end. But that way of thinking can be a double-edged sword: the life of the flesh, fed by the fruit of the tree of the knowledge of good and evil, leads down one path, which is vain and futile; and the tree of life directs us down another, where the true answer lies. To achieve such a lofty aim as being like Jesus, it is critical that we see the difference. That indeed it is the renewing of our mind that must take place if we are to be transformed from our old life to our new one.

The fallen soul—which, remember, took over after the garden failure and became as god itself, knowing good and evil—always has its answers to questions like the one we are considering here. It seeks and begins to list all the many things we must do (and not do) in order to be like Jesus. A famous book called *The Imitation of Christ*, written by a fifteenth-century monk, Thomas a Kempis, follows that pattern. I have no intention of disparaging the book (it has many valid points); in fact, except for the Bible, it has been translated into more languages than any other book in history. Divided into four parts, it sets out to list and explore several steps or disciplines toward the goal of imitating Christ.

It is quite clear from the titles of those four sections of his famous book what a Kempis had in mind: "I. Helpful Counsels of the Spiritual Life," "II. Directives for the Interior Life," "III. On the Interior Consolations," "IV. On the Blessed Sacrament." In addition to a Kempis, both Saint Augustine and Saint Francis of Assisi realized the central significance of being conformed to the image of Christ. Augustine saw it as the remedy for the sins of Adam, and St. Francis believed in both the physical and spiritual imitation of the life of Jesus, advocating a life of poverty and preaching like Christ. For a Kempis, it was a path of imitation based on a monastic withdrawal from the world.

I am certain all three of these spiritual giants realized the enormous role and importance of the Holy Spirit in the transforming and conforming processes, but they all laid at least an equal importance on the outward life as a means to achieve their purpose. And while the outward life does have significance, it should not be overstressed; if the inward moves, which the Word emphasizes take place, the outward will follow. On the other hand, if the inward changes do not occur, the outward matters little.

It is noteworthy that a transformation is required if there is to be any conformation. Romans 12:1–2 calls this transformation a "renewing of the mind," a different way of thinking. The mind, being the main agent of the soul, enters life in a fallen condition. And much of what is learned in this world only complicates the problem. That is why in the Romans passage, we are admonished not to be conformed to this world and its way of thinking, which has been built and dominated by the power and the life nourished by the tree of the knowledge of good and evil.

Certainly, the rational mind of mankind is unique, and one of the attributes that separates us from all other forms of life. But the rational mind cannot reach God! And it must not take precedence over faith in the Word of God. Just think of all the truths of the Spirit that would have to be rejected because the rational mind simply cannot accept them (Romans 6:6, 11, for example). The mind makes a fine steward but a poor regent!

We know that to worship God, we must do so "in spirit and truth" (John 4:24). That is why the Holy Spirit gives us a new spirit at our rebirth. And our spirit operates by faith, believing the Word and the Holy Spirit who reveals or illuminates the Word for us. Sometimes that Word "makes sense" to us, but at other times, it does not. But giving precedence to faith over absolute reason is a key transformation that must take place if we ever hope to be conformed to the image of Christ.

For many years after my conversion to Christ, I walked the path of doing, in hopes that the doing would lead to a change of being. I took classes in biblical theology and systematic theology in an effort to get a better grasp of the Bible. Those were indeed helpful classes, but better understanding of the Word, combined with all my other efforts (much prayer, church attendance, giving, helping, etc.), did not result in much real change. I refrained from known sin as best as I could, repenting when I failed (which was quite often!), but progress in my inward spiritual life was slow at best. In time, I grew frustrated and even angry with God. Eventually, this led to a crisis point.

Outwardly I continued to do the same "good" things, but inwardly I was miserable. My failures at righteousness caused deep feelings of guilt and condemnation. Enter Satan. The enemy began to remind me that my former life of sin at least was pleasurable, a lot better than constantly trying to please God and failing. I cried out to God, telling Him I could not live in that way any longer; I was quitting.

I had one besetting sin at the time, one which I would conquer for awhile, but one way or the other, it always tripped me up again. When I finally realized I could not overcome it in my own power (and was ready to completely throw in the towel), the Lord did a remarkable thing: He took it away! Not only not doing it, but even the desire to do so was suddenly gone. I was amazed! But it took me some time longer to realize that this was not only applicable to this one isolated situation—rather to my entire Christian walk.

Coming to this understanding required the Holy Spirit to show me a number of other truths, which He was faithful to do. Once I experienced victory over that stumbling block of a sin, I was ready to dig back in. Of course I continued to struggle in other areas of my walk, but that one revelation and supernatural experience kept me going. It was that life-changing.

The next step was discovering (the Holy Spirit uncovering!) the difference between our spirit and our soul and the need for the two to be divided (Hebrews 4:12). The Lord showed me that the fallen soul controlled what Romans 6:6 calls the "old man" and that trying to overcome sin and live a righteous life by the power of the soul was doomed to failure; and actually, in so doing, it places one back under the old law! What utter futility: using a corpse to do the work of the Spirit!

The next revelation had to do with being *in* Christ, which helped me understand the reality of being crucified with Christ, and beyond that, the truth of my coresurrection and ascension with Christ, spiritually sitting in heavenly places with the Lord—that once in Christ, always in Christ so that where He has been, I have been, and where He is, I am.

The Lord then revealed to me God's eternal purpose: that His Son, Christ Jesus, would be what the Bible calls "all in all" or in other places in Scripture, "the sum of all things." As I began to explore the meaning of that short phrase *all in all*, I began to realize the full scope of such a purpose. The Holy Spirit taught me that this means God's eternal purpose is for everything that exists to be filled with nothing but the Life and glory of Christ! Filled, no room for anything else!

What we are left with, in the wake of such a revelation as this, is a sense of complete wonder and the nagging question, but how? How do we make this incredible purpose an accomplished reality in our own life? I knew I could not rely on my own efforts; all my previous attempts to imitate Christ had taught me that. I knew I had been given a new spirit and a new heart, and that to commune with God the Holy Spirit, it had to be from His Spirit to my spirit. And He had certainly been unfolding many marvelous things to me. So I waited and prayed and prayed and waited.

I had previously read what Paul called the mystery of the ages, never revealed until the Holy Spirit revealed it to him. I am referring, of course, to the Word that declares that Christ is *in* us, that when we are reborn, He actually comes to dwell within us, a fact that Paul calls the hope of glory. So we are in Christ, and He is in us. I had certainly read this before, but it suddenly came to life for me. If Christ is to be all in all, then surely His Life within must be released; this was the conclusion the Spirit gave me.

We know that Christ never exercised His own will independently of God, but that He always surrendered His will to the will of the Father. If that was the way He lived, we must do the same: submitting our will to the will of

Christ within us. In that way, His Life is released, and He is indeed all in all in such a process. And it is His Life that is ever victorious. So our part is simply submission to and cooperation with the will and Life of Christ.

This is the "exchanged" rather than changed (self-improvement) life to which we are called. We do not lose our own life in such an exchange; rather, we are willing to surrender it in favor of the will of Christ. This is the only way that man is able to be conformed to the image of Christ and Christ to be all in all. Any other approach is doomed to failure. The moment we assert ourselves independently of the will of Christ, we will fail, and Christ will cease being all in all.

It certainly takes much work of the Word, the cross, and the Holy Spirit for God to achieve such a purpose in our life! The Holy Spirit must apply His Word and pierce it deeply into the heart and spirit of a believer, and the cross must do its work of cutting away at the flesh and dividing soul from spirit. It is a slow and painful process, but if we submit and cooperate, the desired end will be reached. The Lord will truly prove His promise in Matthew 5:6: "Blessed are those who hunger and thirst for righteousness, for they shall be filled." We will be filled, and the Lord will be glorified. Thank You, Lord!

CALLED TO PURITY

If you love Me, keep my commandments.

John 14:15

He who has My commandments and keeps them, it is he who loves Me. And he who loves Me will be loved My Father, and I will love him and manifest Myself to him…if anyone loves Me, he will keep My word; and My Father will love him, and We will come to him and make our home with him. He who does not love Me does not keep My words.

John 14:21, 23, 24a

Therefore you shall be perfect, just as your Father in heaven is perfect.

Matthew 5:48

Blessed are the pure in heart, for they shall see God.

Matthew 5:8

To live as He lived, a life of purity and being unspotted by the world, Christ calls His disciples to also live. Matthew 5:8 even exhorts us to be perfect as our Father in heaven is perfect. If we are not careful, such commands and admonishments will set us on the road that leads from the tree of the knowledge of good and evil to failure and frustration. As we have discussed in previous chapters, such a life is impossible if it depends on our natural strength and willpower. Only Christ within us has lived (and can live) such a life.

Therefore, once again, what is called for is the submission of our will to the indwelling Lord. Only He is perfect! It is the Life of Christ that must be released for true purity and righteousness to manifest in our life. All other efforts, no matter how well intentioned, will fall short. Fifteen hundred years under the law of Moses is more than ample proof of this fact. For under the works of the law, none were justified. This was the whole reason for the coming of Christ, to do for man what man was unable to do for himself.

The Lord will allow us to fail again and again in our own efforts to live a life of purity and thereby please Him. He desires us to see that such a thing is not possible. So like Paul's quandary in Romans 7, at times we will do the things we wish not to do and not do the things that we wish to do. But also like Paul, we must come to see that the only solution (as in all situations!) is Christ. For He has set us free from the law of sin and death by living within us and operating by the law of the Spirit of Life, a higher law that has overcome the lower one under which man has lived since the Garden of Eden. But His Life and that law must be released in order to work.

Jesus also linked obedience and purity to love by saying quite plainly that if we love Him, we will keep His commandments, which said another way would be, "If you don't keep My commandments, don't say that you love Me because you don't." Wow! Jesus certainly says it like it is! But again, how does this work? Paul certainly loved Christ in Romans 7 when he was having a hard time with obedience in all things. This was even after his declaration in Romans 6 that his old man had been crucified with Christ.

What Paul lacked until Romans 8 was an understanding of how Christ in us, the hope of glory, actually manifests Himself—by the law of the Spirit of Life! This revelation came to him in the first two verses of Romans 8 after he reached a very dark place of futility and condemnation, as he cried out in desperation, "O wretched man that I am! Who will deliver me from this body of death?" (Romans 7:24).

If we truly love Christ, that love will constrain us in the matter of willful sinning. The sins that once brought us pleasure, or perhaps even bound us, we will no longer wish to do; for in committing those sins, we know we will bring dishonor to the One we love and who loves us. And that mutual love should and will become more important than anything else in our life. Still, as admirable as this is, we need the operation of the law of the Spirit of Life in order to successfully carry out our intentions.

Matthew 5:8 declares that the "pure in heart" will be blessed by "seeing" God. Our old heart, the one we had before salvation, was untrustworthy, for Jeremiah 17:9 declares, "The heart is deceitful above all things, and desperately wicked; who can know it?" That is the very reason we needed a new heart, and indeed the Holy Spirit gave us one at the moment of our regeneration. The new heart is able to work with the new spirit so that we might obey God. I have often thought that the new heart acts as a sort of bridge between the spirit and the mind so that a believer can truly understand a revelation from the Holy Spirit and thereby act upon it. That may or may not be true.

But the new heart is critically important in our walk of faith, so it is critical that it remains pure and unadulterated by the things of the flesh and the world. We must not subject it to those influences. Rather, we must, inasmuch as possible, saturate it with the things of the Spirit: prayer, the Word, and godly associates and conversation. Philippians 4:8 puts it this way: "Finally, brethren, whatever things are true, whatever things are noble, whatever things are just, whatever things are pure, whatever things are lovely, whatever things are of good report, if there is any virtue and if anything praiseworthy—meditate on these things."

Seeing God, the blessing for the pure in heart, is interesting to consider. Certainly, the pure in heart will see God in heaven and eternity, but I believe more is included in this blessing. Receiving and understanding more and more about God now, in this life, is also a wonderful blessing, and one that the pure in heart is given. A pure heart is able to discern what God reveals through His Word and other moments of divine insight and guidance. A partially darkened heart (one that is not kept pure), on the other hand, often misunderstands what God is saying. This false understanding often leads to false teaching and a life that departs from the true path of God. Many have fallen here, even those who in the beginning sincerely sought God. So beware! Do all you can to keep your new heart pure.

The world system, built by Satan and fallen flesh, is the chief obstacle to purity of heart and life. We are surrounded by sin and the temptation to fall to it ourselves everywhere we look in twenty-first-century America. We have truly become a nation of extreme decadence: from drug addiction to rampant consumerism to the beckoning of sex on television (and even in the lingerie departments of leading retailers!) to legalized abortion and gambling. And what is even worse is that so much of it has become accepted!

But then, "the world" has ever been an enemy of the Spirit. That is why we hear this scathing indictment by the apostle John:

> Do not love the world or the things in the world. If anyone loves the world, the love of the Father is not in him. For all that is in the world—the lust of the flesh, the lust of the eyes, and the pride of life—is not of the Father but is of the world. And the world is passing away, and the lust of it; but he who does the will of God abides forever.
>
> 1 John 2:15–17

The words of Paul in 2 Corinthians 6:17–18 put it this way:

> "Therefore, come out from among them and be separate," says the Lord. "Do not touch what is unclean, and I will receive you. I will be a Father to you, and you shall be my sons and daughters," says the Lord Almighty.

Help us, O Lord, that we be pure of heart and deed and not be a friend of the world and its ways!

CALLED TO REST

Come to Me, all you who labor and are heavy laden, and I will give you rest. Take my yoke upon you and learn from Me, for I am gentle and lowly in heart, and you will find rest for your souls. For My yoke is easy and My burden is light.

Matthew 11:28–29

There remains therefore a rest for the people of God. For he who has entered His rest has himself also ceased from his works as God did from His.

Hebrews 4:9–10

And we know that all things work together for good to those who love God, to those who are called according to His purpose.

Romans 8:28

Learning to rest in God is a crucial calling in our life in Christ. Unless we understand and enter His rest, we will continue to struggle throughout our walk with the Lord, remaining outside many of His promises. Yet despite the great need for this state of divine rest, there are apparently few who truly find it. So let's investigate and see if we can discover exactly what is involved here, lest we miss this tremendous blessing of God ourselves. The definitive chapters on what is meant by resting in God are to be found in Hebrews 3 and 4.

The author of this book (most believe it was Paul) starts out in chapter 3:1, reminding us that we are "partakers of the heavenly calling"; and again in chapter 3:14, we are referred to as "partakers of Christ." In chapter 3:6, we are called the "house" Christ has built. These are marvelous things to consider! Of course, there are conditions attached to such precious promises; they are indeed conditional promises. We must "hold fast the confidence and the rejoicing of the hope firm to the end" (Hebrews 3:6). In other words, we must believe and continue to believe what God has spoken.

Paul then makes us acutely aware of the difficulty of continuing such faith. He uses the example of the nation and people of Israel, saying they never entered His rest. In spite of His words, promises, and many miracles when the Lord delivered them from Egypt, the children of Israel fell in unbelief. They simply could not combine their faith with what God had said and done. As a result, all who left Egypt except Joshua and Caleb died in the wilderness on their way to Canaan and never made it to the Promised Land.

Hebrews 4 begins by saying, "Therefore, since a promise remains of entering His rest, let us fear lest any of you seem to have come short of it." It is a deep desire of the Lord that we all enter His rest! After repeating the reason for Israel's failure—unbelief, the Holy Spirit through Paul gives a discourse on just what this rest is all about. To do so, He refers back to the story of creation in Genesis. On the seventh day, God rested "from all His works" (Genesis 4:4). Within this explanation of God resting is the meaning of our rest in Him. But what does the apostle mean here?

Certainly, God was not tired and in need of rest after the first six days of creation! No, the reason for Him "resting" was His absolute confidence that all He had planned and created was perfect, that all His purposes in creation would be successful. After the sixth day and His creation of man, God surveyed all He had made and declared it not only good but "very good." Knowing all things, He knew that in spite of all the many failures, delays, and detours along the way, all that He purposed would come to pass! Nothing Satan nor man would do could abort its success. In this divine assurance, He rested.

(I also believe that when Christ announced, "It is finished!" as He died on the cross and gave up His spirit to the Father, the Lord *saw* the same thing as God saw on the seventh day of creation. He looked down through the ages to come and was able to rest even as He died knowing nothing could prevent the eternal purpose and plan of the godhead from succeeding.)

What does this have to do with us? Everything! For we are to enter that same rest and not allow anything to dissuade us from it. The children of Israel faced many trials and difficulties on their forty-year desert journey; their faith in the Word of God was tested over and over again. And they failed. In this world, our faith in what God has said and promised will likewise be tested. The last thing Satan wants is for anyone to enter the rest of God; such believers are extremely dangerous to him and his survival as the prince of this world.

In my book *Pilgrimage*, I discuss these deterrents to rest by the enemy at some length. The point here is to know that they will come. Without going into detail, some of these deterrents include the world and its prince, circumstances arranged by Satan (and allowed by God), sin, unbelief, fear, pride, sickness, financial difficulties, even our own family— the complete list indeed is long, and our enemy will tailor his tactics to whatever he thinks will secure his desired end. But if we truly believe God and such promises as Romans 8:28, we won't be derailed. For we must come to know and believe that all things do happen for our good, whether we understand them or not. The Holy Spirit, remember, is conforming us to the image of Christ, and even He learned obedience through the things which he suffered. Some of that conforming process is painful and difficult to understand.

Jesus came as a man and endured all the trials and temptations (and many more!) that we face as humans. But he overcame them all, sinning not, and then defeated Satan and death. And as we have said repeatedly, He comes to live inside us! He who said it is finished and did finish it all; that victorious Life is now within the spirit, soul, and body of all who put their faith in Him: Christ in us, the hope of glory!

Actually, before the coming of Christ, no one could truly enter the rest of God. With their spirits unregenerated, they were confined to the frailty of their fallen souls, even in their worship and attempts to do the will of God. The soul in its own power can never do the work of the Spirit; at some point, it will always fail. The unrenewed mind and the natural will and emotions are always defeated by Satan. That is why the children of Israel, under the law, could never enter God's rest. Their souls were not able to overcome doubt, fear, and unbelief when adversity came.

For all believers, this same thing continues to pose a problem. That is why the writer of Hebrews tells us that to enter the rest of God, we must cease from our own works, even as God ceased from His works on the seventh day of creation and rested. Our own works are the works of the soul, originating from us and not from God. That is why Jesus said in Matthew 11:28 that He would give us rest for our souls, for it is all our soulish work and worries that make us weary and heavy-laden! Trying to do the work of the Spirit, the soul will quickly become exhausted! For that malady, Jesus promises to give us rest.

In addition to the admonition to cease from our own works (the first step), two more clues of how to enter the rest of God are given, one in Matthew 11:28–29 and one in Hebrews 4:12. It is crucial that we see these two points. First of all, Jesus tells us that the rest we are seeking, He will "give" to us. It is not something we can earn; it is a gift from the risen Christ. He then invites us to take His yoke upon us and learn from Him. What is His yoke, and what is it we are to learn?

I believe His yoke is the will of God, to which He always yielded. To do so, He had to be meek (gentle) and lowly in heart (poor in spirit), which we too must be willing to do. Submission, as we said before, is the opposite of pride and rebellion, the very cause and result of original sin. These are to die with the old man, crucified on the cross in Christ. If they do not, we will continue to struggle and never enter the rest of God. My admonition? Allow the cross, the Word of God, and the Holy Spirit to break you of all pride and soulishness. His yoke is easy and His burden light only if we submit to His will as He submitted to the Father's will in all things. If we do, the yoke is easy because He has done (and will do) the work. If we do not, the yoke is impossible, and the burden will crush us!

How is it that He breaks us and brings us to completely rest in God? If we truly believed that the old man, with all his failures and deficiencies, died on the cross with Christ and lived the reality of that incredible fact, no breaking would be necessary. But it seems that vestiges of the soul life of our old man hang on and cause serious problems in our efforts to live a spiritual life, at rest in the Lord. The apostle Paul wrestled with this same issue (see Romans 7), and I am sure, even after seeing that the law of the Spirit of Life has overcome the law of sin and death (the law of the old man), that the struggle surfaced again from time to time.

Hebrews 4:12 gives the solution to the dilemma:

> For the word of God is living and powerful, and sharper than any two-edged sword, piercing even to the division of soul and spirit, and of joints and marrow, and is a discerner of the thoughts and intents of the heart.

We see in this passage that there is a need for soul and spirit to be divided, to become separated so that the soul ceases to be involved in the work of the spirit (except as a steward carrying out the will of the Spirit). Of course, the cross and the Holy Spirit must get involved as well, the cross through the Word doing the necessary surgery to the flesh, and the Holy Spirit giving the revelation of the Word so that the mind is renewed. This is an ongoing process throughout the lifetime of a believer and is called in the scriptures *sanctification.*

Even though some pain and suffering in the flesh accompanies the division of soul and spirit, and the soul often resists, we must come to a place of rest in God even in this operation, knowing that it is for our good and God's glory. It is the very way in which we become conformed to the image of Christ and our creation, as God intended it to be, completed. As we decrease, so to speak, the Life of Christ increases and is released to manifest itself. Knowing this should be more than enough to rest in what God is doing. And the more we enter His rest, the more we experience being "partakers in Christ," partakers of His divine nature, the "house" in which Christ is welcome and abides.

So my prayer is that none of us fails to enter into His rest, for there is the place of refuge, safety, and power! Life in this world will continue with its challenges, and the enemy will not relent in his attacks, but hopefully, this promise of rest still available will sustain and give us reason to persevere. Persevere and rejoice—and again, I say, rejoice! Amen.

CALLED TO LEAVE THE WORLD

My kingdom is not of this world.

John 18:36a

Of judgment, because the ruler of this world is judged.

John 16:11

Do not love the world or the things in the world. If anyone loves the world, the love of the Father is not in him.

1 John 2:15

For the earnest expectation of the creation eagerly waits for the revealing of the sons of God...because the creation itself also will be delivered from the bondage of corruption into the glorious liberty of the children of God. For we know that the whole creation groans and labors with birth pangs together until now.

Romans 8:19, 21–22

The wolf also shall dwell with the lamb, the leopard shall lie down with the young goat, the calf and the young lion and the fatling together; and a little child shall lead them...They shall not hurt nor destroy in all My holy mountain. For the earth shall be full of the knowledge of the Lord as the waters cover the sea.

Isaiah 11:6, 9

Now I saw a new heaven and a new earth, for the
first heaven and the first earth had passed away.
Also there was no more sea.

Revelation 21:1

If you were of the world, the world would loves
its own. Yet because you are not of the world, but
I chose you out of the world, therefore the world
hates you.

John 15:19

"Therefore come out from among them, and be
separate," says the Lord. "Do not touch what is
unclean, and I will receive you."

2 Corinthians 6:17

To be in the world but not of the world is a most difficult
position to maintain. At every turn and by every means,
the world (and its prince) strives to draw us in. We are
surrounded by beckonings of the flesh and inundated with
the allure of sin. What we continually see and hear is hard
to ignore. We cannot turn on television or go outside our
door without the world offering its tempting morsels to our
baser appetites, from scantily clad females to the constant
imploring cries to buy more and more stuff we don't really
need. (Truly, the blessings of God have turned to curse in
modern America!)

The apostle John exhorted us to love neither the world
itself nor the things of the world and that the whole world
lies in the evil one. He goes even further by saying that if
we do love the world, the love of the Father is not in us.
Those are extremely harsh and condemning words but true

nonetheless. When I addressed this subject in one of my books, a young man who read it emailed me, saying that he had tried not to love the world but had failed: "For when I go outside and behold the beauty of nature," he said, "I find that I really do love it after all."

Of course, the young man misunderstood John's exhortation and my writing. We are not to hate the natural creation, the beauty and the splendor of nature. We are to love it, even as God loves it (John 3:16) and was willing to send His Son to die for it (as well as for us). For with the fall of man came the fall of the world, neither as God had intended them to be. Creation itself is waiting to be renewed (Romans 8:19–22), even as we who are in Christ have already been renewed, born anew from above.

In its current fallen condition, the world is the product of Satan and fallen man. Men have unconsciously endeavored to restore an Eden-like world, a return to the garden, so to speak, but such efforts will never succeed. For the world has already been judged and is passing away. The old creation can no more be repaired than the old man; both have been condemned to death. Both will be replaced by a new creation, first mankind and then the world. In fact, the Word declares that the only delay for the renewal of the world is the manifestation of the sons of God (Romans 8:19).

Christ said that we cannot serve both God and mammon (money), that we would either love the one and hate the other or vice versa (Matthew 6:24). Money is closely related to the things of the world. In itself, money is not a bad thing. Although I believe it is a creation of Satan and fallen man, a certain amount of money is required to purchase basic necessities. If our use of it stops there (with an occasional "hyacinth for the soul" perhaps), we have not fallen prey to its deadly attraction. But its danger, of course, lies in its appeal to avarice and the pampering of the flesh. The more we have, the more we seem to need the money and the pleasures it can bring. Many are the believers of Christ who have failed here. The pursuit of money, the things it can buy, and the false sense of security it engenders become great obstacles and distractions to the pursuit of godliness. Soon, God fades to the background in such lives. It is this that we must guard against happening to us.

The fact that Jesus declared that His kingdom is not of this world (John 16:36) should be enough to turn us away from the current world as well. For if His kingdom is not of this world, neither is ours. We await and eagerly anticipate His return and the establishment of His kingdom, the true kingdom of God on earth. We know from scripture that we shall rule and reign with Him in the new kingdom for a thousand years and that we shall be like Him and see Him as He is. Hallelujah! What could be better than this?

We do not have a clear description of what the earth will look like during the millennial reign of Christ. But surely it will undergo a beautification process: all pollution cleaned up, rivers renewed, plentiful crops and food, cities rebuilt, free of slums and poverty, etc. The earth will also be free of the ravages of Satan and fallen angels, for they will be confined in a bottomless pit for the entire millennium. There will yet be flesh-and-blood human beings on the earth, as well as the glorified overcomers in Christ. Life expectancy will be greatly increased among the mortals, but death will still occur, as will some sin. For the Word says in Isaiah 65:20, "No more shall an infant from there live but a few days, nor an old man who has not fulfilled his days;

for the child shall die one hundred years old, but the sinner being one hundred years old shall be accursed."

The humans yet in mortal bodies who live during the millennium will also have to make a choice for Christ if they are to be part of the new heaven and new earth (eternity). After a thousand years have passed, Satan and his hosts will be released for a short time and will still be able to deceive many! This in spite of the fact that they had been prevented from directly tempting anyone for the duration of the millennium. Those who choose Christ will be saved, but those who refuse and go the way of Satan will be cast into the lake of fire, along with Satan, demons and fallen angels, death, Hades, and all not found written in the Book of Life. This is all related in the twentieth chapter of Revelation.

The glory of the Garden of Eden would have been a wonder to behold! But as glorious as it was, I believe the splendor of the new earth spoken of in Revelation 21 and 22 will exceed Eden. And mankind will be more excellent beings than Adam and Eve. For all things will be as God originally ordained them to be—perfect! The eternal purpose will have been accomplished: all creation will be filled with nothing but the Life and glory of Christ!

As we read about the millennial reign of Christ and the new heaven and new earth, we realize just how far this world has fallen and the great need for its rebirth. We see repeatedly in scripture that Satan is called the prince and ruler of this world. This is the world we are not to love, the world system that has been created by Satan and fallen men. How long it will be before Christ returns? No one knows. But in the meantime, we are to live as foreigners and pilgrims in this world, knowing this is not our home.

Even as the prophet Daniel in Babylon, we too are exiles in this world, awaiting our release. While we wait, with the help of the Holy Spirit and the indwelling Christ, we must be vigilant and careful about our contact and conversation with the world. We must remain untainted by it, unspotted from it (James 1:27). We must listen and heed the Word, which says,

> And what agreement has the temple of God with idols? For you are the temple of the living God. As God has said, "I will dwell in them and walk among them. I will be their God, and they shall be My people. Therefore come out from among them and be separate," says the Lord. "Do not touch what is unclean, and I will receive you. I will be a Father to you, and you shall be My sons and daughters," says the Lord Almighty.
>
> 2 Corinthians 6: 16–18

Even so, come quickly, Lord Jesus!

CALLED TO EXCHANGE LIVES

Knowing this, that our old man was crucified with Him, that the body of sin might be done away with, that we should no longer be slaves to sin.

Romans 6:6

But God, who is rich in mercy, because of His great love with which He loved us, even when we were dead in trespasses, made us alive together with Christ (by grace you have been saved), and raised us up together, and made to sit together in heavenly places.

Ephesians 2:4–6

When He had called the people to Himself, and His disciples also, He said to them, "Whoever desires to come after Me, let him deny himself, and take up his cross, and follow Me. For whoever desires to save his life will lose it, but whoever loses his life for My sake and the gospel will find it."

Mark 8:34–35

I affirm, by the boasting in you which I have in Christ Jesus our Lord, I die daily.

1 Corinthians 15:31

> I have been crucified with Christ; it is no longer I
> who live, but Christ lives in me; and the life which
> I now live in the flesh I live by faith in the Son of
> God, who loved me and gave Himself for me.

Galatians 2:20

Any sincere seeker after Christ and the true life in Christ must eventually come to the end of himself; if he does not, he will never find what he is so desperately seeking. The soul is the main obstacle in such a search, especially the mind and its limits of rational thinking. The mind must awaken to the reality that there is something quite beyond itself, something that simply cannot always be grasped by thought. All would agree to that outright, and yet our minds still slow most of us in our spiritual pursuits and progress.

That is why the mind must be renewed, made new in the sense of accepting by faith all that is written in the Word of God. Certainly, God is a God of reason, for He invites us to come reason together with Him (Isaiah 1:18). But His reason is a higher reason, divine reason, one which we will better understand in our future glorified state. However, even then, reason will not take precedence over faith, and we must not allow it to do so now. Actually, the most reasonable thing we can do is believe whatever God says; it is unreasonable to believe anything else!

Emotions can also be a hindrance to our search for true spiritual life. Many today gauge whether God is in a message, times of prayer, or reading the Bible by emotional experiences, how it makes them feel. From the seeing of visions to prophesying to being "slain" in the Spirit and a myriad of other ecstatic experiences (many of them unbiblical), feeling takes the lead in such believers. If anyone objects on the basis of the Word, they are often quickly dismissed and accused of legalism.

There are two dangers in this approach to God: Satan himself can influence emotions, giving false emotional highs and convincing the recipients that what has transpired is indeed from God. This can be a dead-end to spiritual progress, such believers thinking they have reached the pinnacle of growth in God and remaining there. The second problem is that no experience or thought must ever contradict or nullify what God has spoken in His Word; only what He has said is authentic truth. Hear the Word near the very end of Revelation:

> For I testify to everyone who hears the words of the prophecy of this book: If anyone adds to these things, God will add to him the plagues that are written in this book; and if anyone takes away from the words of the book of this prophecy, God shall take away his part from the Book of Life, from the holy city, and from the things which are written in this book.
>
> Revelations 22:18–19

A most sobering declaration!

The other culprit of the soul is the will. Along with the mind and emotions, our own will has been in charge of our life before coming to Christ, and those three faculties do not automatically relinquish control once we come to believe unto salvation. They merely attempt to refocus their operation, striving to do "good" instead of sinning. The will is ever busy in this endeavor, vowing to no longer waste time in trivial or sinful activities but instead to replace these with Bible reading, church attendance, prayer, etc. While such resolutions are indeed good ones, alas, they do not lead to what we are looking for. Instead, spiritual progress does not accelerate, certain old sins hang on, and eventually we become stagnant and frustrated in our walk.

But if we do not give up and continue to hunger and thirst after righteousness, the Lord will keep His promise and come to our rescue again and again, filling us with what we need next (Matthew 5:6). It may be the illumination of such verses as Mark 8:34–35, where the Lord tells His disciples and others who were present that to find their life (*psuche*, soul), they must lose their life for His sake and that they must be willing to deny themselves, take up their cross, and follow Him.

Or it might be Romans 6:6 and 11 where Paul declares that our old man is dead, having been crucified with Christ. The Holy Spirit might then link these two passages together so that we come to see that the fallen soul life and the old man are one and the same! The acceptance by faith that these two words are true (in spite of loud protests by reason!) causes us to wonder what this "new" soul might be like and how it differs from the old soul.

We might then "chance" upon Hebrews 4:12 where it states that the soul and the spirit must be separated by the Word of God. This comes as an extremely crucial revelation: like Paul in Romans 7, we too have experienced continued difficulty in the areas of obedience and godliness. We know that our old man (old soul life) is dead, but something continues to go wrong as we "reckon" this to be so. At times, our failures are even worse than before!

And on and on it goes, the Lord supplying exactly what is needed next to clear the soulish debris from our path. The order and ways in which the Holy Spirit teaches these essential truths (as He guides us into "all" truth as promised) vary with each individual believer, but all the means He employs are designed and implemented to take all of us to the same end or goal: to conform us to the image of Christ and to make Him all in all in our life.

What I began to see was that my new spirit was to ascend and my soul descend to the role of being a servant or steward of the Spirit via my spirit, no longer leading the way or being in control. Being the pivotal point between spirit and body, however, the new soul's function is extremely important: my mind must understand what the Holy Spirit is saying through His Word so that my will can be triggered in His desired direction. But of course, the will must be surrendered to the will of the Spirit of Christ even as the will of Christ was surrendered to the will of the Father; in that way, His will can truly become our will, and our will His will.

In addition to the mind being renewed and the will surrendered, the emotions are certainly also brought into play. As we worship and obey the will of God, basking in His glory, our emotions overflow with gratitude and praise, a key to both glorifying and enjoying the Lord now and forever! As the Holy Spirit does His work within our spirit, with our mind and will following in obedience, our emotions are truly overjoyed by the wonder and goodness of God.

As I began to walk in this way, I also began to notice that I seemed to have more peace and less worry, less guilt and feelings of condemnation, and more confidence and trust in the Lord, remembering His words that He would be with us always and never forsake us. I began to enter what Hebrews 3 and 4 call the rest of God, knowing that whatever came from His hand in my direction (no matter how difficult it might be) was for my good and His glory. Rather than quickly trying to pray unpleasant circumstances away, I tried to discern by the Spirit why they had happened, what the Lord was trying to teach me. When the Holy Spirit answered my inquiries, the situation almost always worked its way out! When it did not, I realized it was just an attack from Satan that could be cast off by prayer.

As I began to "rest" in this way, I also noticed that the indwelling Life of Christ would often be released in very surprising ways. Rather than just a natural knee-jerk reaction to some situation, I would react quite differently. At times they seemed to make little sense; I didn't even understand why I had responded in such a way myself. But often, by the results that followed or what the Lord was trying to accomplish, I came to see that it was exactly the correct response.

About this time, I encountered the concept of an exchanged life, the Life of Christ becoming our life. I think the idea was introduced to me by the writings of Hudson Taylor, a British missionary to China in the nineteenth century. As I studied about it and prayed, comparing my own experiences and understanding of the scriptures to those of Mr. Taylor, I was delighted and more and more convinced that such a conclusion was indeed correct. I had already seen that Christ is to be all in all and the sum of all things in our life. However, no matter how hard I strove to make this a reality in my life, I failed. But as I said before, the more I was able to rest in the Lord, the more that it seemed to be Him coming forth and not myself. Furthermore, we know that He exchanged His Life for ours when He died in our place on the cross. Are we not now therefore to exchange our life for His in return? This was the way my thinking and spirit were drawn in those days, and it has persisted to be the way that I have gone ever since.

I have not found anything about an exchanged life to be contradicted by the Word; rather, I have found much to support it. How else can Christ truly become all in all in our life without being released and being so? Anything else would be a mixture, and He would cease to be all. We know that our old man was crucified with Christ, but what about our new man? How is he to live and avoid going down the same path as the old man? And how else can we explain Paul's unequivocal statement, "I die daily" (1 Corinthians 15:31)? He can only be speaking of the new man in Christ, there being no need for the old man to die again and again. Paul "died" so that Christ might live!

And what else could Paul mean in Galatians 2:20 when he declares it is no longer he who lived? Here is the full wording of that glorious declaration:

> I have been crucified with Christ; it is no longer I who live, but Christ lives in me; and the life which I now live in the flesh I live by faith in the Son of God, who loved me and gave Himself for me.

In the part 3 of my book *Pilgrimage: Finding the Way Back Home*, I discuss this matter of an exchanged life in much greater detail, but I hope I have said enough in this chapter for you to understand and for your interest to be piqued enough to investigate further for yourself. It is my belief that all believers are called to an exchanged life, ours for His. And in order for such a marvelous transformation to come about, it takes work by the Word, the cross, the Holy Spirit, and our surrender and cooperation with what the Lord desires to do. In the next chapter, we will discuss the call to overcome, which I hope will further clarify how only an exchanged life leads to full maturity in Christ and a victorious life.

So cease from your own works of trying to please the Lord and be more and more like Jesus. Such a thing is simply not possible or necessary: you are in Christ and He is in you. That is more than enough!

CALLED TO OVERCOME

This is the word of the Lord to Zerubbabel: "Not by might nor by power, but by My Spirit," says the Lord of hosts.

Zechariah 4:6

Thus says the Lord to you: "Do not be afraid nor dismayed because of this great multitude, for the battle is not yours, but God's."

2 Chronicles 20:15

Then all the assembly shall know that the Lord does not save with sword and spear; for the battle is the Lord's, and He will give you into our hands.

1 Samuel 17:47

These things I have spoken to you, that in Me you may have peace. In the world you will have tribulation; but be of good cheer, I have overcome the world.

John 16:33

And to the angel of the church in Philadelphia write, "These things says He who is holy, He who is true, He who has the key of David, He who opens and no one shuts, and shuts and no one opens: I know your works. See, I have set before you an open door, and no one can shut it; for you have a little strength, have kept My word, and have not denied My name. Indeed I will make those of the synagogue of Satan, who say they are Jews and are not, but lie—indeed I will make them come and worship before your feet, and know that I have loved you. Because you have kept My command to persevere, I will also keep you from the hour of trial which shall come upon the whole world, to test those who dwell on the earth. Behold, I am coming quickly! Hold fast what you have, that no one may take your crown. He who overcomes, I will make him a pillar in the temple of My God, and he shall go out no more. I will write on him the name of my God and the name of the city of My God, the New Jerusalem, which comes down out of heaven from My God. And I will write on him My new name."

Revelation 3:7–12

Many believe that everyone who has been born again will take part in the millennial kingdom, that to be one who has been saved by grace is enough to be qualified to enter. I have difficulty with that belief. Certainly, all the redeemed will be part of the new heaven and new earth and eternity; nothing can prevent that. But to rule and reign with Christ during the millennium is not a free gift; it is earned. It is a reward for those who overcome in this life. All believers are not overcomers.

Salvation is by grace through faith alone. It is a gift; where is the overcoming in that? All are saved by grace alone, but reward is on the basis of works after salvation. We have already established that man must cease from His own works (those that originate in his soul and not his spirit); the Word describes all these as "filthy rags" (Isaiah 64:6). So what are the works that will be rewarded by being part of the millennial kingdom?

Jesus answered His disciples when they asked him what were the "works of God" by saying, "This is the work of God, that you believe in Him whom He sent" (John 6:29). To believe in Him, of course, means more than just belief that He is the Son of God who came to save men from sin and hell; we must also believe in everything He said. This includes such declarations as "Apart from Me, you can do nothing" (John 15:5). And lest we think that means that we must simply call on Jesus to help us in our time of need, we must remember that John 15 relates the parable of the vine and branches. The vine does not merely help the branches to survive; the vine is the very source of life for the branches, a life they both share.

This realization is further proof that without an exchanged life, the Life of Christ becoming our life, there is no way to overcome in this life and take our place during the millennium. As in all parables, the comparison of the vine and its branches being a perfect picture of Christ and believers breaks down at a certain point: The branches of the vine need not go through any change to receive nourishment from the life of the vine. We, on the other hand, have the blockage of soul (self) that must be removed in order for the Life of Christ to flow.

Many other statements appear in both the Old and the New Testaments concerning how it is that we overcome Satan, sin, and the tribulations of this life. In John 16:33, after warning His disciples of what would happen once He was delivered up, He concludes by telling them, "These things I have spoken to you, that in Me you may have peace. In the world you will have tribulation; but be of good cheer, I have overcome the world." Wow! After telling them of all the terrible things that would happen to them after He departed, He says for them to be of good cheer, and that He has only told them that they might have peace! Facing such dire warnings (which indeed did come to pass), how could peace and good cheer even be possible?

The peace, good cheer, and being unafraid are to be explained by two assurances that accompanied the warnings: His disciples (and we) are "in Him," and He has already overcome the world! And not only are all believers *in* Christ (and cannot be taken out), but He who has already overcome dwells within us; meaning that since He has overcome, so can we. We simply must allow His Life to be our life, and victory is certain (not to mention peace and good cheer in the midst of battle!).

In the Old Testament, the children of Israel were delivered again and again, not by their own strength but by the power of the Lord. In Zechariah 4, 2 Chronicles 20, 1 Samuel 17, and many other places, victory over great odds came because the Lord intervened on behalf of His people. The cry of the Lord was always the same: the battle was His, and therefore not by their might or power, but by His Spirit would they be saved. Our Captain is ever so much more powerful. For He has not only won the battle, He has won the war!

The parable of the ten virgins in Matthew 25 only makes sense if we understand that it is a picture of who will attend the wedding supper of the Lamb (during the millennium) and who will not. All ten were virgins and had oil in their lamps, hence all belonged to the Lord (unbelievers are never spoken of as virgins, nor do they receive the oil of the Holy Spirit). All ten waited for the coming of the Bridegroom. But then a problem developed: the Bridegroom delayed His coming, and the lamps of the foolish virgins began to go out. The wise virgins had plenty of oil, having with them vessels of extra oil.

The extra oil of course could not be shared with the five foolish virgins. This was not a case of the wise virgins being selfish; this becomes clear as we ask ourselves what the extra oil represents. What was the basis of the ten virgins being divided into two groups of five? The answer gets to the crux of the matter concerning grace and reward, being part of the new heaven and new earth but not part of the millennial reign of Christ.

The extra oil was given to the wise virgins each time they denied self and allowed the Life of Christ to be released for the challenge at hand. The foolish virgins received no extra oil because when confronting similar situations, the cost to self seemed too high, and they were unwilling to pay it. Some Bible scholars have insisted that the five foolish virgins were either not saved at all or were saved but then lost their salvation since they were not allowed to attend the marriage supper. But neither of these ideas is correct: we have already established that all ten virgins belonged to the Lord, saved by grace, their salvation not based on works. Therefore they could not lose their salvation due to their failure to work.

My conclusion: all ten virgins were saved, all bound for heaven, but only five of them were qualified to attend the marriage supper during the millennium. Salvation is by faith through the grace of God, but reward is based on what we do after salvation.

Revelation 2 and 3 speak of this very subject. Seven churches undergo inspection by the Lord Himself, during which He speaks of both the strengths and weaknesses of each. For the weaknesses, there is only one remedy: repent! Some of the failings are not only deficiencies but are outright sin and rebellion! But all of those sins can be traced back to men, and not God, being in charge. Once the soul begins to try to do the work of the spirit, all sorts of distortions, aberrations, and blemishes appear.

Rather than examining each church, let us focus on the one which seems to be the model church, the one with which the Lord finds no fault: Philadelphia. It seems to be a small gathering, not particularly strong, but there are three salient features that the Lord commends: they had persevered, kept His word, and not denied His name. In spite of the attacks by the enemy and the tribulations of the world, they had not given up; they had "kept His word and not denied His name" (Revelation 3:8, 10). They had been able to persevere because they had relied on His Life for victory in their troublesome circumstances, thereby keeping His word and in this way had not denied His name, for His name is who He is!

As a result, the believers at Philadelphia are given great and precious promises as their reward for faithfulness. They will not only be part of the millennium, ruling and reigning with Christ, but they will also be spared from going through the great tribulation. And then after that, they will be made a pillar in the temple of God forever! Hallelujah! These saints are true overcomers.

Now it is our turn. We too are called to be overcomers. And after forty years of being a follower of Christ, it has become clear to me that the only way to overcome is to

exchange our life for the Life of Christ, to allow the Word
and the cross to cut away at our flesh (including our soul)
until nothing remains that will be a hindrance to the release
of His Life.

Before He went to the cross, Jesus asked an incredible question:

> Nevertheless, when the Son of Man comes, will He
> really find faith on the earth?
>
> Luke 18:8

Certainly, He will find the faith of those who have
believed unto salvation and will go to heaven. But will he
find the faith of the overcomers, faith like the overcomers
in Philadelphia, who will rule and reign with Him in
the kingdom?

CALLED TO THE KINGDOM

In those days John the Baptist came preaching in
the wilderness of Judea, and saying, "Repent, for the
kingdom of heaven is at hand."

Matthew 3:1

From that time Jesus began to preach and to say,
"Repent, for the kingdom of heaven is at hand."

Matthew 4:17

Your kingdom come, Your will be done on earth as
it is in heaven.

Matthew 6:10

And this gospel of the kingdom will be preached in
all the world as a witness to all nations, and then the
end will come.

Matthew 24:14

Many students of the Bible believe that the millennial
kingdom and heaven are one and the same; the fact that
the term *the kingdom of heaven* often occurs only serves
to complicate things. Certainly, when Christ returns, in a
sense, heaven will also be here, for wherever Christ is, it will
be heavenly. But I still strongly believe that the two realms

must be clearly distinguished from each other. If one insists on calling them both heaven, I have no problem with that, but surely we can also agree on the division of heaven into two separate and distinct manifestations: first, the thousand-year reign of Christ on earth and then the new heaven and new earth that will follow and endure forever.

We are called to both, to be saved by the grace of God and to be overcomers once salvation is secured. This chapter will only deal with the call to the millennial kingdom. To speak of this call, it is impossible not to include the call to an exchanged life and the call to overcome; there will therefore be much overlapping of these three calls as we proceed to consider the call to the kingdom.

Some have called the book of John the new Genesis because both books open with the words *in the beginning* and both books deal with similar themes and contents. But the book of Matthew is the first book in the New Testament, even as Genesis is the first in the Old Testament, so we can assume that its positioning is important, that God's intention is to emphasize something of primary interest to Himself (and therefore to us).

Some have called the book of Mark the account of Christ as the suffering servant; the book of Luke, Christ as the perfect man; and the book of John, Christ as God. Those are very good distinctions and are quite warranted by the contents of the three books. What then is the book of Matthew all about? How does it depict Christ? The book of Matthew presents Christ as king and is therefore the book of the kingdom. The coming of the kingdom therefore is central in the mind and plans of God.

From before the creation of the worlds, in eternity past, the Father's eyes have been on the kingdom. Hence, after the first two chapters of Matthew, in which the writer details the royal lineage of Jesus and then speaks of His miraculous birth as foretold by the prophets, followed by a snapshot of His early years in Egypt and Nazareth, John the Baptist is brought into the story, announcing the coming of the kingdom. (Even the genealogy of Christ confirms that the book of Matthew is about Jesus as king and the coming of His kingdom, for Matthew's list begins by calling Jesus the Son of [King] David, the Son of Abraham, and not tracing His line back to Adam as does the book of Luke in its third chapter, Luke emphasizing the manhood of Jesus.)

John the Baptist was a special instrument of God. He was the forerunner of Christ, the herald who would both prepare the way and announce the coming of the Messiah. When we first meet him in Matthew 3, John is about his divine business, preaching in the wilderness of Judea and declaring for all who would hear him, "Repent, for the kingdom of heaven is at hand." Isaiah had prophesied concerning John, and this is mentioned as confirmed prophesy in Matthew 3:3:

> The voice of one crying in the wilderness: "Prepare the way of the Lord; make His paths straight."
>
> Isaiah 40:3

John was also baptizing those who would confess their sins, not the baptism of forgiveness but the baptism of repentance. When he beheld Jesus, in the Spirit, John recognized Him as the promised Messiah; and after some reluctance, John consented to baptize the Lord. Jesus had nothing from which to repent, but as He explained to John, His baptism was required so as to "fulfill all righteousness"

(Matthew 3:15). Jesus came as the representative man, a substitute for all mankind, so it was right and proper that He should be baptized in our place, for all of us have sinned and come short of the glory of God.

Immediately after His baptism (and God speaking from heaven, confirming the Sonship of Jesus), the Lord was led into the wilderness by the Spirit to be tested by the devil. In another of my books, I have spoken in detail of the three temptations Jesus faced, but for our purposes here, let us confine ourselves to a single point: Christ succeeded by depending on the Word of God and the Life of the Father within Him. He did not react on His own, from His own soul. Obviously there is a great lesson for us here.

The next thing to notice is that after His baptism and testing, overflowing with the Holy Spirit and victorious over the enemy, Jesus began for the first time to preach. And what did He preach? "Repent, for the kingdom of heaven is at hand" (Matthew 4:17). So John the Baptist came announcing the arrival of the kingdom, and it was the first thing Jesus preached. Later on in Matthew, when the first apostles and disciples were sent out, they also preached the same message of the kingdom. And in Matthew 24:1, Jesus declares, "And this gospel of the kingdom will be preached in all the world as a witness to all nations, and then the end will come." It's not just the message of salvation, but this gospel, the gospel of the kingdom. From all this, it should be apparent how focused God is upon the kingdom. If that is His focus, should it not be ours as well?

Two important points should be mentioned before we proceed. The first concerns an understanding of what John and Jesus meant when they said, "For the kingdom of heaven is at hand." To be at hand means already here or about to come. Two thousand years have come and gone, and as many skeptics point out, neither has Jesus returned nor has heaven appeared (implying of course that this proves the Bible is not inerrant). I have to admit that I was bothered when I first read these words many years ago. But later on, hopefully with some growth in understanding, I understood what John and Jesus were saying.

We usually speak and think of heaven as a place far off where all believers will someday go. But the Holy Spirit has taught me that heaven (at least for now) is anywhere and at any time Christ truly becomes Lord of one's life; for those, spiritually speaking, the kingdom of heaven has already come! When John first spoke those words, the kingdom was at hand because the King was at hand; and if one accepted Him as both Savior and Lord, the conditions for "heaven" were met. The same is true today. Certainly, someday believers will dwell forever in a place called heaven, but the kingdom of heaven is not limited to time or geography; it is available now!

The second point to be made is the erroneous idea that it is the church that is building the kingdom. Actually it is the other way around: the kingdom is building the church. The book of Matthew speaks of the kingdom over fifty times, and the church is mentioned twice. As we just said, the kingdom has come when the King is present and ruling. With no King, there is no kingdom; and without the kingdom, there is no church! (The same thing is true of our misunderstanding of the word *pastor*, which is mentioned only once in the New Testament, and yet we have made him the head over local churches. But that is a completely different topic, so we won't go there for now!) It is the kingdom that is foremost in the mind of God, His kingdom coming to earth so that His will might be done here as it is in heaven. The church is to be the expression of His kingdom.

But just what will the kingdom look like? Both the Old and New Testaments give us pictures of the kingdom, each from different perspectives. The Old Testament concerns itself mainly with the Jews and therefore their part in the kingdom. There will be Jewish people in the kingdom and in the heaven to come, but they will be what are commonly called "completed" Jews, those who have come to Christ. The prophet Daniel speaks of the coming kingdom, a time in which all the promises made to the descendants of Abraham, Isaac, and Jacob will be fulfilled concerning inhabiting all the land promised to them by God. This promise will come to pass during the millennial reign of Christ.

But in the New Testament, we see two other perspectives on the kingdom: the first is to be found in what is called the Sermon on the Mount in Matthew 5, 6, and 7. In this discourse by Jesus, what is stressed is the character of those who will inhabit the kingdom. In the Beatitudes (Matthew 5:3–12), the Lord gives the sterling qualities of those who will be blessed in the kingdom. A careful reading of those virtues, compared to our own lives, leaves only one plausible conclusion: only Christ Himself is capable of such high standards. But this is exactly what the Lord wants us to see! We cannot live up to the conditions of the Beatitudes; only the Life of Christ within us being released can succeed.

The other place to look for a slightly different view of the kingdom is in the parables. The parables give what the kingdom would look like from the outside looking in. That is why the parables often begin with just those words:

"in that day the kingdom shall be like or likened to." In the parables, we see the fulfillment of the promise made to the church, whether they be Gentile or Jewish believers: "To him who overcomes I will grant to sit with Me on My throne, as I also overcame and sat down with My Father on His throne" (Revelation 3:21). This promise will be fulfilled first during the millennium, for a thousand years, and then in the new heaven and earth forever.

When the Bible declares that nature itself is waiting for the manifestation of the sons of God, it seems that the character of those who will inhabit the kingdom is of paramount importance. As we said, these character traits are listed in the Beatitudes; and until they come forth, neither the internal or external qualities of the kingdom matter—the people are the crux of the matter. Until they appear and manifest, I believe the coming of the kingdom will be delayed. For that to happen, we must rely on nothing but the Life of Christ within and learn to live by it.

O Lord, it is my earnest prayer that Your people will begin to see the glory of Your kingdom, and that its glory will be so magnificent in their hearts that their primary desire becomes to see its coming. And that they might understand their part in it and so live to hasten its coming. In the name of Your Son and our Lord, amen.

CALLED TO HASTEN HIS COMING

The Lord is not slack concerning His promise, as some count slackness, but is longsuffering toward us, not willing that any should perish but that all should come to repentance. But the day of the Lord will come as a thief in the night, in which the heavens will pass away with a great noise, and the elements will melt with fervent heat; both the earth and the works that are in it will be burned up. Therefore, since all these things will be dissolved, what manner of persons ought you to be in holy conduct and godliness, looking for and hastening the coming of the day of God?

2 Peter 3: 9–12

The apostle Peter begins this chapter of his second letter reminding us of the words spoken before by the holy prophets and by the apostles themselves and to stir us up with what he has to say. He starts by giving a prophecy himself: in the last days there would be scoffers, "walking according to their own lusts" (2 Peter 3:3). Their argument would be the same one mentioned earlier, by asking, "Where is the promise of Him coming?" (2 Peter 3:4). Why such a long delay?

Peter answers such objections by stating that indeed things have changed since the beginning, and then he lists a few of those changes. Next he gives the reason for the delay: God is not willing for any to perish, so in His long-suffering, He has given men the opportunity to repent and come to Christ. But he reminds those skeptics that all the Word has said will come to pass, including the earth and all the works in it being burned up exactly as foretold.

Peter then turns his attention to believers by asking how it is we should live in light of what is coming. His answer? To live holy lives, looking for and hastening the coming of the Lord. I remember the first time the Spirit illumined this passage for me. Hasten His coming? You mean we can actually hasten the day of His return? I was astounded! And the Spirit made this very clear as well: you can also delay His coming. Do you see what a responsibility that places upon us?

After I recovered from the initial shock of that revelation, I realized I must better understand what constitutes a holy life. The answer to that question is what this book and my others are all about. I had already realized that I was unable to live a holy life myself (as defined by God). Jesus hinted at that when the rich younger ruler addressed Him as good teacher, and Jesus said, "Why do you call me good? No one is good but One, that is, God" (Matthew 19:17). If no one is good, then certainly no one is holy but One. This story is told in Matthew, Mark, and Luke, so the Lord thought it important enough to repeat.

If no one is holy but God (Father, Son, and Holy Spirit), then the only way we can live holy lives is by Him manifesting. And He will do so! By our willing surrender and cooperation with the indwelling Life of Christ. By doing that, we will hasten the coming of the Lord; and by not doing it, we will delay His coming. O that we might come to see that and live accordingly!

Up until now in the history of Christianity, I am sorry to say that most of what has transpired has delayed and not hastened the Lord's return. The soul and the ways of man have invaded the spiritual realm, much to the delight of its instigator, Satan. Men have transformed the church into an organization, much like the corporate patterns of business. Instead of operating as a body under the leadership of the one head, Jesus Christ, a hierarchical system has been put into place. Decisions are made by democratic vote, usually going the way of "leadership."

A better understanding of the Greek words for bishops, deacons, elders, etc., is much needed: those roles in the first-century church, which should be our pattern, were mainly in the areas of support and service, not leadership. In the body of Christ, each member has a function to fill for the edification of the whole body. In a properly functioning body, there would be no need to vote: the Holy Spirit would make His wishes known, and the body would carry them out.

Churches should be intensely local, not part of a huge organization where all local churches are to follow what was decided at headquarters. This insures that any errors made would also be localized, not disseminated to other bodies. When the apostle Paul made visits to various churches to see how they were doing and then wrote letters to those churches, they were free to listen to Paul and make the recommended changes or they could ignore him. He did not dictate how things should be or call for a vote.

And in Acts 15, when a dispute arose over the need for circumcision and keeping the law of Moses (in other words, to pass from Judaism to Christianity) in order to be saved, the council that met debated the issue—listening to

Paul and Barnabas tell of many Gentiles being converted to Christ in the course of their ministry. They were also reminded of Peter's experience at the house of Cornelius. There was no vote taken, but when the Holy Spirit revealed His will in the matter, they were all of one accord.

So many things have gone awry that the Lord wishes to correct. But the answer to the problems does not lie in us trying to fix what is wrong. The answer is the same as in all things of the Spirit: Christ! Even a small number of local believers can shake the world again if Christ is allowed to be released. There is much talk in the church today about revival, and there is certainly a great need for one. Not a copy of what has happened before, and certainly no counterfeits, full of sound and fury but signifying nothing. What I long for is the final revival, one in which the Life of the Lord emerges and manifests among His people, one that will hasten and herald His coming, truly preparing the way of the Lord.

But it all starts in individual hearts. Hearts that hunger and thirst for the Lord. Hearts that will sacrifice all things for His return. Hearts that are no longer content with the lukewarm, a form of godliness with no power. Hearts that are eager for the fulfillment of prophecy and the Word. Nothing else will make any lasting difference—just another bell-shaped curve that will have to repeated again in the future.

Maranatha!

SUMMING UP

Why in the world am I here? Beginning with that basic question, which all mankind answers one way or another, whether it be worded and consciously sought or simply answered by the way life is lived, we have come full circle. We started with the *Westminster Confession of Faith*'s answer—to glorify God and enjoy Him forever—and have explored what God has to say on the subject. We discovered that all men are called by God, initially for salvation, and then, for those who hear and respond in faith to that first call, the callings of life in Christ, a life full of such love and glory that it constrains us to glorify God and rejoice.

We have learned many other things along the way. For me, the most precious of these is the call to experience the love of God. Although His love is something that is only gradually experienced and treasured by most believers, it is what holds all the rest together, the Life in Christ bound by the love of God. All of any spiritual worth flows from His love. To confine such a marvel to words is quite beyond me. George MacDonald, a nineteenth-century writer, poet, lecturer, and great spiritual thinker had this to say in a terse and powerful observation called "Inexorable Love":

> Nothing is inexorable but love. Love which will yield
> to prayer is imperfect and poor. Nor is it then the

love that yields, but its alloy...For love loves purity. Love has ever in view the absolute loveliness of that which it beholds. Where loveliness is incomplete, and love cannot love its fill of loving, it spends itself to make more lovely, that it may love more; it strives for perfection, even that itself may be perfected—not in itself, but in the object...Therefore all that is not beautiful in the beloved, all that comes between and is not of love's kind, must be destroyed. And our God is a consuming fire.

C. S. Lewis, George MacDonald: An Anthology, p. 1

What a perfect and profound description! *Inexorable* means unyielding, relentless, not to be moved, even by prayer or entreaty—and this is how we are loved by God. He loved us while yet His enemy, full of vile rebellion and sin; it was His love that drew us to His Son. After giving us the unimaginable, a new heart and new spirit (and His very Life!), He begins to clean us up and teach us how to walk in the new life He has given us. There are many falls and pains along the way, but they are all designed to remove anything that is not lovable (although He never ceases to love us anyway!). The Word calls this being conformed to His image, the perfect bride of Christ. Once we come to see this and yield to it (the yoke of the Father's will), rest is indeed the result, the yoke made easy and the burden light.

Two stories in scripture come to mind: Solomon's Song of Songs and the parable of the prodigal son. As a man, the prodigal's father never ceased loving him, never ceased praying for him and looking down the road for his return. It was that love that drew the son back home a changed man. If we see the father as a picture of our Heavenly Father, the story and its results remain the same. God allows us to wander to a far country far away, and He allows us to make whatever wrong choices we choose. But He never stops loving us! And it is that love that one day causes us to "come to ourselves" and come back home, where the Father is waiting with open arms and the "fatted calf" to celebrate our return.

The story of the Shulamite maiden and the king in the Song of Solomon has been much misunderstood by even the most prominent Bible scholars. Rightly understood, it is the very heart of scripture: the story of us, individual believers, and the King of kings. Already a believer at the beginning of the story, the maiden longs for more intimacy and love from the king (O, may we never cease longing for this!). It is the outpouring of that love by the king that leads the Shulamite onward. Many trials and areas of flesh to be removed remain ahead, but the inexorable love of the king leads her through them all. By the end of the story, the Shulamite has become a perfect bride for the king. Her story is our story!

For me, the change that takes place in the Shulamite can be best seen in the subtle reversal of how she expresses her love for the king: at first she would say, "He is mine, and I am His." But later this becomes, "I am His, and He is mine." We must be truly loved before we can truly love in return. At first our love may remain a bit selfish (O what the Lord does for me behind the lattice, our secret place!). But as we mature, it becomes reversed. At long last, we have so completely surrendered to the love of Christ that all selfish motives are gone. Whatever comes from His hand we know is for our good and His glory, serving only to increase the love between us.

When all is said and done, this is what we are called unto. A good friend of mine, a brother in the Lord, likes to ask people their definition of God, which can be a difficult question. His definition? God is the one who loves me. I can think of no better definition. And because He truly loves us (inexorably!), we can truly love Him in return. And that is what eternity is all about! Glorify God and enjoy Him forever? Well, I guess!

The One Who Loves Me

God is the One who loves me,
This Father best defines;
Love throughout eternity,
The crown of His designs;

From exile His Son retrieved,
He gave all He possessed;
Spirit ensures love received,
Then blessed and blessed—and blessed!

AFTERWORD

The seed of this book was formed and planted after hearing a short series of messages by Dr. Daren Carstens. The title of the series intrigued me: "Why on Earth Am I Here?" I realized that this is every man's question. And then I was so pleased Dr. Carstens taught that after answering the call to salvation, the first thing God desires for us is to experience His love more deeply. Those two things set the roots, and the Spirit begins to water.

The book is designed to assist those who are already followers of the Lord, to lighten the load and help them along the way, and also for those who are yet outside Christ to be drawn in. For God indeed has called and is calling all men. No other answer to why in the world we are here makes sense and gives any real purpose to life. I hope the book has served its purpose. Know the Lord loves you and wants to make you His own. To that end, I pray that the humanly incomprehensible love of the Father, Son, and Holy Spirit would engulf you and be shed abroad in your heart, that you might come to truly know why in the world you are here: to be loved by God and to love Him in return. For that is the answer to all questions.

My other books published by Tate

"Silly Snake Rhymes...and the real stuff." (children's book)
"From the Garden to the Kingdom: God's
Eternal Purpose, Plan, and Provision"
"Pilgrimage: Finding the Way Back Home"
"Songs of a Son: Heart-cries Along the Way"